THOSE WHOM THE GODS WILL NOT FORGIVE

OTHER BOOKS BY MJ ROWLEY:

Good Friday I

Shadows

THOSE WHOM THE GODS WILL NOT FORGIVE

M J ROWLEY

SilverWood

Published in 2014 by the author
using SilverWood Books Empowered Publishing ®

SilverWood Books
30 Queen Charlotte Street, Bristol, BS1 4HJ
www.silverwoodbooks.co.uk

Copyright © MJ Rowley 2014

ISBN 978-1-78132-190-4 (paperback)

British Library Cataloguing in Publication Data
A CIP catalogue record for this book is available from the British Library

Set in Sabon by SilverWood Books
Printed on responsibly sourced paper

Chapter 1

May 2012

The sound of the air locking system closing the doors behind him sounded to Ronnie like the starting pistol for the next job he'd been thinking about. A job he'd been mulling over for the last couple of years while resident at B wing, Wormwood Scrubs. Carrying a black plastic bag holding the gear handed back to him a few moments earlier Ronnie made his way across the courtyard to the main gates. The warder, unlocking the side door, looked him up and down. "Behave yourself, Ronnie, you're getting too old for this game." Ronnie White was a handsome, rugged looking guy, seventy-one years of age, but still in excellent shape. Six foot two with a perfect physique, he smoked two packs of cigarettes a day but still looked capable of running up Snowdon before breakfast. He glanced over at the warder with a grin. "I could outrun you lot any day of the week." Walking out on to the forecourt Ronnie's girlfriend, Debra Andrews, forty years his junior came running up to him. Flinging her arms around his neck she kissed and hugged him allowing her long silky blonde hair to brush against his cheeks and neck. "OK, girl," said Ronnie, keeping his hands firmly round Debra's slim twenty-six inch waist, and continuing to enjoy the feel of her beautiful body and the aroma generated by a mix of her sensuality and expensive perfume all of which he'd missed so much. "We've things to do, kid, where're you parked?"

"Just over the road, Ron. I thought we'd go back home, have a bath together and, you know, have some long overdue fun. Then we need to get your best gear out. We've got a party organized tonight.

Geoff, Billy, Martin, George and all the boys will be there."

"OK, Debra, love, you drive."

Ronnie threw his bag into the boot of the Audi A5 convertible he'd bought Debra for her twenty-ninth birthday then climbed into the passenger seat. "You'll have to put your seat belt on, Ronnie, otherwise we'll have that sodding bleeping noise in our ears for the next hour or so."

"Bleeding things," said Ronnie struggling with the belt. "Fucking 'ealth and safety wherever you go these days."

Debra smiled, "No 'ealth and safety for us when we get back home though, Ron, love."

Ronnie smiled as he touched Debra's slim thirty-one inch legs. "I should hope not."

Ronnie's career began in the underworld of Soho over fifty years previously. There was not much he hadn't turned his hand to. He'd started out as an errand boy for the Kray twins, worked for a short time with the Richardson brothers and a few others. He was familiar with activities on both the east and west side of the river. He'd even acted as a courier for the KGB at the height of the cold war during the late 1960s. Ronnie was well known and well liked, strangely enough not only by his counterparts but several members of Her Majesty's constabulary. They'd come to know him well over the years; a sort of mutual respect had built up. Ronnie, however, was more than the typical likable rogue. He had both class and brains. He'd built up a well organized and very profitable business he nicknamed 'Counterfeit'. Lookalike Rolex watches, illicit booze, cigarettes and any other items he was able to secure without the annoying encumbrances of VAT, or any of the other charges usually expected by Her Majesty's revenue. He'd managed over the years to almost entirely avoid prison having been a guest of Her Majesty on only two occasions, once in 1978 as a result of a raid on Salloways the jewelers on Bond Street which went terribly wrong, and the second time two years of a four year sentence, now just completed, for VAT and tax fraud. Ronnie thought the sentence was a bit heavy but the Crown Prosecution Service had been able to prove that somewhere in excess of £9m had been omitted from Ronnie's VAT returns. That, together with the fact the labels on the bottles of whisky, vodka and gin were albeit very professionally forged, did not exactly live up to what it said on the tin. After a massive fine and two years of a four year sentence, Ronnie was this morning a free man, and still very solvent. He'd managed to keep a couple of million tucked away in different and very discreet hiding places, but he was ambitious. He enjoyed the challenge of a new scheme, especially one promising a payout in the region of £90m plus. Just before his unfortunate invitation to join the other inmates at B wing, Wormwood Scrubs, two years previously, he'd been given the idea by a long-time associate of his, Franz Zimmerman. Zimmerman was a wealthy and successful businessman, in fact one of the richest men in the country at one time. However, due to the current recession and virtual collapse of the worlds banking system, Franz Zimmerman was looking for ways to improve his cash flow. With the collapse of Lehman Brothers and others, Zimmerman was thought to have lost well in excess of £150m. Like all enterprising entrepreneurs he was looking for ways to repair the damage as quickly as possible, and was quite prepared to diversify. Ronnie, just before his stay at Wormwood Scrubs, had purchased a large five-bedroom property in the Cotswold village of Moreton-in-Marsh just a few miles from Franz Zimmerman's place, Broom Hall at Stow-on-the-Wold. Debra had arranged the letting of Ronnie's pad in Shepherds Bush, and had spent the last eighteen months or so getting their new home in shape. "You wait till you see it, Ron, you won't recognize the place. I've done it just how you'll like it. There are a mix of colours for the lounge; cream walls, white woodwork, and the most beautiful, deep pile gold carpet. There's an out of this world five-piece suite, and the very latest sixty-five inch plasma TV on the wall over the fireplace. The kitchen diner has deep red walls and polished oak flooring. It looks real regal, Ron." Debra went on and on. "And upstairs, in our bedroom..." she giggled. "No, I won't tell you what I've done there. I'll leave that as a surprise."

Ronnie was anxious to get home. A couple of hours with his beloved Debra and a few hours of relaxation followed by a decent meal at his favorite pub, The Kings Arms, were the ingredients needed to complete his journey back to the real world, his world as he called it. Ronnie had spent most of his time making visits to the prison gym and the library whilst at Wormwood Scrubs. He'd not been attracted to the work on offer to inmates paying £1.15 an hour. He laughed at the warder when given the details. "And I thought I ripped people off! I should keep all that under your hat, mate, otherwise you'll end up sharing B wing with the rest of us for exploiting slave labour."

The outline of the plan given to him by Franz Zimmerman involved stealing a consignment of uncut diamonds on their way from Antwerp to Zurich, where eight in ten of the world's rough diamonds were processed. The deliveries were made every six months or so and Zimmerman told Ronnie he could arrange with the security firm involved an easy ride for his guys. No resistance, no guns. Just board the aircraft, collect the containers, load them up and drive away. Had anyone else come to Ronnie with such an idea he'd have told them to get lost, but not Franz Zimmerman. He knew what he was on about. If he said he was able to arrange an inside job then you knew it was for real. Ronnie and Franz Zimmerman went back a long way. It was 1959 when they first came into contact with each other when Ronnie, just nineteen years old, was beginning to carve out what was to be a very successful criminal career. Zimmerman needed money to help finance his electrical wholesale business and this gave Ronnie the chance to move into the big time. Three robberies were planned and with Zimmerman's contacts and guidance, Barclays Bank and two post offices, one at Leamington Spa the other in Solihull, would provide the rewards. Zimmerman provided the outline of the plan and the muscle required which turned out to be six Hungarian immigrants well versed in the art of survival having survived three years of the Russian invasion of their country. Ronnie was the coordinator of the operation, the man on site, the leader. The jobs were successful. Zimmerman got the money he needed, Ronnie got a good share and so began a lifelong association which provided Ronnie with many opportunities and helped make him the success he was today. Whenever Franz Zimmerman had one of his moneymaking ideas he called on Ronnie to work the scheme. Total trust existed between them, which was why Zimmerman had decided to wait for Ronnie to be released from Wormwood Scrubs before embarking on the plan he had in mind. The job was big, even for Zimmerman.

After indulging himself for a couple of hours with Debra in their newly decorated bedroom complete with sunken bath, ceiling and wall mirrors and two enormous TV screens, Ronnie threw on the new black and gold dressing gown Debra had bought him, went downstairs, poured himself a brandy and relaxed in the lounge. "Where do you fancy eating tonight, Deb, the Kings Arms or shall we invite everyone here?"

"I thought we could do both, Ron, it's only just turned four now.

We could shoot down to the Kings Arms at about six and have one of the fillet steaks you love so much, then meet up with the lads back here around nine. You could all talk business in the drawing room which, incidentally, I haven't shown you yet. It's got a bar and full-sized snooker table. You'll love it. The girls and I can keep out of the way in here."

"Sounds OK to me, Deb. You call the lads. Tell them to be here by nine."

After the fillet steak and chips, two pints of bitter and a long welcome home chat with Billy Marks and his wife, who Ronnie had set up in the business some years previously, he and Debra drove back home. The lads arrived at Ronnie's place promptly at nine o'clock. One of the many things Ronnie had always insisted upon from the members of his team was punctuality. This and many other 'rules and regulations according to Ronnie' as the team called them were to be obeyed without question. Ronnie always insisted on the best. To be the best you had to be disciplined. To survive in the world of crime you had to be better, smarter and quicker than those around you. At just after midnight, after several fairly good-natured games of snooker, Ronnie, clearing the snooker balls away, placed in the center of the table a map of Brussels Airport.

"Right, lads, you're looking at where we, in a few weeks time, are going to make a minimum of one million pounds each, Brussels Airport. On the 14th of June an aircraft carrying gold and diamonds will land here on its way to Zurich carrying somewhere in excess of £90m worth of diamonds, and around £10m in gold bullion. Our job is to drive up alongside the aircraft. Dressed as Belgian police officers we board the plane, take off the containers, load them into the vans and drive away. No guns, no resistance, the security firm handling the consignment know we'll be there. It's all arranged."

Ronnie's team, Martin, George, Alan, Billy and Geoff all stared at the map. Geoff, the youngest and the most recent member of Ronnie's team looked up from the table. "Did you say £90m, Ron? How the hell has something like that been arranged?"

"You're working for the professionals now, Geoff. You don't ask questions other than questions relating to your role, and your teams role in the operation. You're not knocking off your local Spar shop now."

Geoff looked slightly indignant as he ran his fingers through his hair. "I just wondered that's all."

Ronnie looked at Geoff with his steely blue eyes. Geoff could be a good and useful member of the team, but he was green. Perhaps, thought Ronnie, this job is too soon for him. He couldn't afford any weak links. He'd need to have Billy Spears keep a very close eye on him. "You do exactly as you're told, Geoff. You look and you learn, young man. And yes it's big, so just remember there's no time for stupid questions and there's no room for mistakes."

Geoff, regaining some of his composure, nodded. "Understood. My apologies."

"OK, lads, now the outline of the plan is as follows. We fly over to Brussels on different flights and dates. Deb will organize the travel arrangements, passports, etc. Alan, you'll be in charge of transport so you and Martin will need to go over a week before and organize that. We'll need two four by fours and a JCB to help cut through the perimeter fencing at the airport," Ronnie, leaning over the map, pointed to the marks he'd made, "just here. We'll need three cars, fast but not flashy, and petrol to get rid of them and everything else when the job's done. As I mentioned a moment ago we'll all be dressed as members of the Belgian police. Deb will sort the uniforms out for us. We park the getaway cars here." Ronnie, leaning over the map, pointed to the second mark he'd made. "There, just over three miles from the airport. You, Alan, will wait with the cars while the rest of us do the business. We cut through the fencing which, with the help of the JCB, will take no more than five or six minutes. We drive up to the side of the aircraft, board the plane, pick up the containers, load them into the truck and drive to where Alan is parked. On the way we cut open the containers and bag the diamonds. The gold we leave at a designated spot on the way, agreed payment for the security arrangements, or lack of them. We change back out of the uniforms, ignite the trucks and drive away. When we get back here the diamonds will be buried away for a while until all the excitement has died down. Then, they'll be cut and eventually sold."

Geoff looked puzzled. "How do you mean, Ron, cut?"

"The diamonds are all uncut. They'll look more like a pile of glacier mints than diamonds, which may be helpful when bringing them back."

"So," continued Geoff, "we have to wait for all that to be done before we cash in?"

Ronnie looked at Geoff. "Any problem with that?"

Geoff, much to the amusement of the other members, stuttered out his reply. "No...no problem at all, Ron. Just wondered, that's all."

In the early hours of a warm, midsummer morning, deep in the heart of one of the most picturesque Cotswold villages, an outline of a plan had been discussed. A plan which was very soon to go down as the biggest and most audacious robbery of all time. However, the chain of events which followed would cause one of the most embarrassing incidents for British intelligence, and pose a serious threat to diplomatic relations between the Kremlin and Downing Street.

Chapter 2

Eleven months later, April 2013

Driving through the typical Monday morning traffic on her way to the station, DCI Sheila Whiteman was not looking forward to the week ahead. She'd no doubt it was going to be one hell of a frustrating time for her and the team. The sub station at Birmingham Central was closing, and the team was moving to the main offices at Steelhouse Lane. Sheila had been based at Digbeth since joining Birmingham Central four years ago. It was reasonably easy to park there which was certainly needed if not essential for Sheila's driving technique, or lack of it. The pub, The Angel and Harp, a two minute walk from the station, proved an invaluable bolt-hole to both her and her team members when in need of a change of scenery whilst attempting to decipher the cryptic, often intricate clues left scattered like remnants in the final chapter of someone's life story it was their task to unravel. The new offices at Steelhouse Lane were, to Sheila, totally characterless, ultra modern, open plan and boring. She would miss the Victorian building they'd all become so used to; the oak stairways and doors, the intricate ceiling roses and cornices, all of which seemed to create a feeling of individuality. Sheila's new office was totally the opposite. Separated by three enormous glass walls, it overlooked the main office with its forty or so desks, computers, filing cabinets, laser printers and fax machines. Some forty or so officers and backup staff made it look like the control center at Cape Kennedy or, perhaps more accurately, thought Sheila, like Tesco's on a Saturday morning. Gone now were the days when she'd be able to retreat to the privacy of her own small office to relax and allow her analytical attributes to work through the problems of the moment. There was, at the new offices, an incident room where her team together with the other officers would meet to discuss progress, or otherwise, on any current investigation. This was where decisions would now be talked through and decided upon in any current investigation. It all felt to Sheila like some very impersonal, mass production exercise. She'd need to find a new routine for herself very quickly, an escape program, away from all the modernization of procedure so enthusiastically pursued by the new generation of management so sure of their doctrine. A bit like the banks, she thought to herself. They got rid of the managers dismissing any real human contact or understanding, then replaced the whole system with call centers and computer-generated programs before eventually going bust. She was not going to allow that to happen to her. She was good, one of the best. She knew it, so did others, she'd just need to make the point a bit more often And she would. God help anyone who thought they would change her way of working. Sheila smiled to herself, "I'll get Greg to sort them out." DI Greg Williams, ex army, and probably the best copper around, next to her, she thought.

After negotiating the multi-story car park at Birmingham Central, Sheila took the lift to the ground floor and walked through to reception. Superintendent Davies was there talking with one of the officers. A stickler for boring procedure, but when the chips were down he could show a very different, creative and determined side to his character which Sheila had discovered last year when involved in the investigation of the murder of Franz Zimmerman. That investigation, ten months later, was still ongoing. A total of eighty-six bodies had been discovered at Broom Hall, all illegal immigrants murdered by the aforementioned in the 1970s after he'd sold out his factory at Long Marston and no longer had use for them. Franz Zimmerman, once believed to be the head of the so-called Knights Templar organization, had been guilty of organizing and financing racial attacks throughout Europe. Documents recently made public named a number of high profile members of his organization including politicians, bankers and two large commercial organizations, revelations Whitehall had been somewhat unsuccessful in their efforts to keep buried.

"Good morning, Sheila, a new dawn for Birmingham Central, all under the same roof now. When you've settled in come and see me.

I need to go over one or two things with you. I'm on the fourth floor. Sergeant Manning will show you."

"Right, sir, as soon as I've sorted a few things I'll be over."

"By the way, are the others here yet?"

Sheila, looking at her watch that showed seven fifteen, doubted that Greg was even out of bed. "Not sure, sir, only just arrived myself. They might be upstairs. If not they'll be here soon."

"Well come and see me when you've got yourselves sorted out."

Sheila took the elevator to the second floor and walked through into the open-plan office. Yes, she thought, as she made her way across to her office, just like Tesco's on a Saturday morning. She was introduced to everyone; all but two of the new DCs she'd met before. Everyone seemed pleased to see her; not, however, DI Goode. He was the ambitious, jealous type, and didn't like the competition. Forty-two years of age, thin, balding, a weedy-looking individual with a nasty side to him, and not liked at Birmingham. Sheila had already sussed him out. Best to avoid him, she thought, for the time being anyway.

Twenty minutes later, Sheila, busy sorting through all her papers in need of filing away in her new office, looked up to see the elevator doors opening. Amidst an array of bad language which seemed to be referring to the multi-story car park as something designed to test the patience of a saint, DI Greg Williams arrived. Strolling across to Sheila's office, Greg made his usual entrance without knocking. "Where've you parked, Sheila? You've never made it up that open air block of flats we're supposed to park in have you?" Sheila had worked with Greg for three years and was used to his outbursts, bad language and cavalier attitude. She took no notice. She allowed him space and simply benefitted from his excellent work as a DI, his friendship and remarkable loyalty. She was perhaps the only person, certainly in the force, who'd been able to train the great oaf. Not only train him, but get the very best from him.

"OK, Greg, lets get all the language out the way. We've work to do here, and we have to get ourselves familiar with everything."

"Already done my bit, Sheila. I've told the desk sergeant there's no fucking way we're all negotiating that stupid car parking arrangement every morning. You, me, George and Ryan now have allocated parking spaces on the ground floor at the back of reception just as you drive in."

"Well done, Greg. Now stop moaning and help me put all these files in the cabinets will you?"

Sergeant Ryan put his head round the door. "Morning, everyone. What do you think of the new offices so far?"

Sheila gave Greg one of her looks and said, "Don't answer that."

"The Super's just asked me to give you this, Sheila. A nurse at the QE has been found dead this morning. Shot through the back of the head apparently, at his apartment. One of the neighbours discovered him about an hour ago."

"Right, Sergeant, you carry on getting settled in here. Greg and I'll drive over and take a look." Sergeant Ryan handed Sheila the report and went out to the main office to carry on sorting out his desk.

"We can take my car," said Greg, "I've moved it behind reception in the spaces we've been allocated. I'll show you, come on."

Chapter 3

Due to an accident at Five Ways Island, it took Sheila and Greg just over an hour to reach their destination, Raddlebarn Court, White Acre Road, a typical late 1960s apartment building five minutes drive past Birmingham University and the Queen Elizabeth Medical Center. Greg pulled into the car park behind the apartment block. Walking up to the main entrance Sheila held up her warrant card to the constable standing there.

"Good morning, ma'am. The pathologist and some of the forensic team are already here, apartment seven, just upstairs on the first floor."

"Thank you, Constable." Sheila and Greg ascended the stone stairway with its light blue painted metal handrail, then along the corridor to apartment seven. The door to the apartment was partly open. Sheila could see the pathologist, Brian Stevens, kneeling beside the body of a man lying face down in the hallway just a couple of meters from the door.

"Morning, Sheila, I take it you had the same problems we encountered this morning?"

"The traffic, Brian? Yes, not only the rush hour but an accident apparently at Five Ways. You have a look around, Greg, while I see what Brian can tell us."

"One shot to the back of the head would have killed him instantly," said Brian. "Time of death around midnight, and from what the neighbour told the constable downstairs I understand she discovered the body this morning. Apparently the door had been left half open. She caught a glimpse of our man here as she was leaving for work. As no one heard any noise, or gunshot last night, it's my guess a silencer was fitted. We'll know for sure once I've examined the bullet. Brian got to his feet. "This has all the marks of a professional hit."

"You know, Brian, you wouldn't make a bad detective," said Sheila.

Brian smiled, "I thought I already was."

Sheila stared down at the body, attempting to visualize the last few minutes of his life. Why the hell was a nurse working at the Queen Elizabeth Medical Center shot through the back of the head by a professional hitman?

Greg was looking around the apartment. In the lounge the television had been left on; there was a half-filled glass of red wine on the table next to the armchair. The kitchen, thought Greg, was in an even worse state than his. About a week's collection of cups, plates and cutlery, all waiting to be washed, and an empty Chinese takeaway carton on the worktop next to a half open packet of biscuits. The bedroom wasn't much better. The double bed looked as though it hadn't been made for a week, probably longer. The wash basket in the corner of the room overflowed with clothes in need of a visit to the launderette. On the bedside cabinet Greg saw what looked like a building society passbook. It was. An account in the name of Stephen Milligan. The Coventry Building Society, account opened on the 15th of August 2011 with a cash payment of £25,000. Regular withdrawals since had reduced the balance, as of the 18th of March 2013, to a mere £25.

"Anything, Greg?" asked Sheila as she came into the bedroom.

"Looks like he'd been watching television," Greg replied, "then, someone calls and puts a bullet through his head. Television left on, glass of wine by the chair in the lounge. Forensic are going over everything so we'll have to wait to see what they come up with. This might be interesting though." Holding up the passbook Greg turned to Sheila, "Twenty-five grand paid in, in cash, on the 15th of August last year. All gone now apart from £25. A bit unusual don't you think for a nurse on around £27,000 a year?"

Sheila flicked through the pages. "Could have been a win or something, gambling, horses, but you're right, it could be interesting. We'll get Sergeant Ryan to take a look at this and all of Stephen's finances. It looks to me that Stephen Milligan could have been shot by someone he knew."

"How do you work that one out," asked Greg as he followed Sheila out to the hallway.

"He was shot in the back of the head a couple of meters from the front door. Now if someone calls to see you, you answer the door, and if it's someone you know you'd probably just tell them to come in. You would then turn round and make your way back to the lounge. If the caller was someone you didn't know, or didn't know that well, you'd be more likely to hold the door open for them then close it behind them before showing them through to the lounge. So if the killer was known to Stephen, he answers the door, tells whoever it is to come in, starts to walk back to the lounge…"

Greg, interrupting said, "Then gets a bullet in the back of the head."

"It's possible," said Sheila. "Get a statement from the neighbour Brian tells me discovered the body. Then, while we're waiting to see what forensic can tell us we need to make contact with Stephen's next of kin. Meanwhile get Constable Finmore to do a door to door. We need to know everything and anything about Nurse Milligan, how long he's lived here, visitors etc, then we'll have a word with his colleagues at the QE."

Brian, coming in from the kitchen, looked at Sheila. "Well, my work here is done. I'll catch up with you later with my report."

"Any idea how long that will take?"

"Should get it finished later this afternoon, Sheila, barring any unforeseen developments. I'll ring you as soon as I've finished."

"Thanks, Brian." Sheila turned to Greg, "Right, Greg, after taking a statement from the neighbour who says she discovered Nurse Milligan this morning, get everyone together in the incident room this afternoon, four o'clock, we need to agree a way forward on this."

Chapter 4

The incident room at Birmingham Central was almost twice the size of the main office Sheila and her team had been used to at Digbeth. Several side cabinets surrounded the walls and three large noticeboards. A center table surrounded by twelve chairs, but no coffee percolator, thought Sheila, as she sat down and put the file on the shooting of Nurse Stephen Milligan on the table in front of her. Sitting around the table was DI Greg Williams, DS Ryan, DC Finmore and DS Peters, who'd moved to Birmingham Central from Digbeth some twelve months earlier, and two detective constables who Sheila had not worked with before, a Maureen Evans and Christine Williams, and at the end of the table DI Goode, the one member Sheila was going to have to keep her eye on. Opening the file, she began. "OK, everyone, the shooting of Nurse Stephen Milligan. Thirty-seven years old, had worked at the QE Medical Center for the past five years. His body identified this afternoon by his parents. Stephen was shot in the back of the head at his apartment sometime between twelve midnight and one o'clock this morning. The pathologist confirms he was shot with a .38 caliber pistol and, as originally thought, verifies it had been fitted with a silencer. Stephen was found in the hallway of his apartment at seven twenty this morning by the neighbour at apartment eight when she was leaving for work, an Alison Moore. Greg, you interviewed her earlier, what can you tell us?"

"Simply that the front door to Stephen's apartment had been left slightly open. Alison saw Stephen's body as she walked past on her way to work this morning. She'd not heard any gunshot or any other noise from Stephen's apartment last night. The only thing she did hear was a door closing downstairs. It woke her up at about one o'clock. Not an unusual occurrence apparently, she told me she was a fairly light sleeper and was often woken by tenants coming and going. But she heard nothing from Stephen's apartment at all. She told me he'd been living next door to her for a number of years. They'd got on quite well, very well in fact. She'd described him as the perfect neighbour. She confirmed Stephen was gay, had a boyfriend living with him up to about twelve months ago, also a nurses at QE, Andrew something, she couldn't remember his full name. She was unaware of any falling out when Andrew moved out of Stephen's apartment. In fact he'd been calling on Stephen quite regularly recently. They often went out for a drink or a meal together."

"And, Constable Finmore," said Sheila, "you carried out a door to door at the apartments. Anything you can tell us?"

"I've spoken with all but two of the tenants," said Finmore. "They all gave pretty much the same comments as Stephen's next door neighbour. No one had a bad word to say about him. There's no CCTV at the apartments so we need to run a check on those nearby. That part of Birmingham, I know, is very busy so that'll probably take some time to get through, but we need to look at absolutely everything at the moment."

"Sergeant Ryan, you've been doing your usual digging. Anything of interest?"

"Well, yes, as it happens. The building society passbook Greg found shows £25,000, in cash, being paid in twelve months ago. I think I know why he opened a separate account for this. His bank statements confirm he'd had an overdraft of £2,500 which from March 2012 had steadily increased over the past twelve months to £3,800. Recent letters from his bank confirm they were asking for this to be reduced. Three cheques sent out last month by Stephen had bounced including one he'd sent to the managing agents who've confirmed Stephen was three months in arrears with his rent payments."

Sheila looked across at the team. "So has Stephen's murder got to do with money, or his mismanagement of it? He's certainly proved, from what we can see, to be rather careless in that regard. He opens a building society account last year with a cash payment of £25,000 then twelve months later all that has gone, and not only that his personal overdraft has increased by £1,300, and he's three months behind with the rent. The withdrawals Stephen had been making from the building society account, Sergeant, were any of them cheque payments?"

"No, all cash withdrawals."

Sheila shrugged her shoulders. "That doesn't exactly surprise me." Sheila was thinking, leaning back in her chair.

"Could this be drug related, Chief Inspector, or blackmail?" It was DI Goode who put the question.

"A good thought, Inspector, it could be either. At the moment though, we look at everything. We need to find out, firstly, more details on Stephen's financial arrangements and, secondly, a lot more about him, his friends, habits and weaknesses so, DI Goode, perhaps you'd start by having have a chat with his parents. Try and find out who is friends were; speak with them. Let's get to know this man. Find out everything you can about him. I'm going over to the QE to have a chat with his colleagues to see what, if anything, we can learn there. Let's all remember the first forty-eight hours of a murder investigation are invariably the most important, so I want you all back here tomorrow at midday. Let's see what we can find out by then."

Everyone began leaving the room. Sheila turned to Greg, "OK, let's go and see what Stephen's colleagues can tell us at the QE. You can drive." The traffic, whilst heavy as always along the Bristol Road, was much easier than the morning run. Finding a parking spot at the QE, however, was not.

"One of the largest and most comprehensive medical centers in the country," said Greg. "Just a pity they forgot about making the parking arrangements easier."

Twenty minutes later, after walking along what seemed like miles of corridors and stairways, Sheila and Greg met up with Charles Maycroft, the human resources manager. He was a short, bespectacled man, late forties, receding hairline and spotted complexion. Just the sort who'll keep on talking about nothing, thought Sheila. I do so hope he doesn't.

"Terrible news, Chief Inspector, I heard it on the lunchtime news. I just can't believe it. Stephen was so well liked by everyone. Hard-working, and a very capable nurse. Who'd have done such a thing?"

"That's what we're determined to find out. Did you know him well?" asked Sheila as they continued walking along what seemed like another unending corridor.

"Not personally, Chief Inspector, as you'll no doubt appreciate the trust employs almost seven thousand staff. It's not possible to get to know everyone. What I can do is introduce you to Stephen's ward sister who should know more about him. Stephen has been working in A & E, the accident and emergency ward. He's been there for just over eighteen months now." Charles pointed to a sign on the wall at the end of the corridor which Sheila could just make out. "It's down here at the end of the corridor." Arriving at the entrance of the A & E Department, and after wiping their hands with the antiseptic gel from the wall dispenser outside, Charles rang the bell. After a few moments the door was opened by, noticed Greg, a very attractive lady. Late thirties at a guess, he thought, blonde hair, lovely complexion, blue eyes and a great figure. Charles introduced them. "This is Maureen Entwhistle, the ward sister. Maureen, these people are from the police who are investigating the death of Stephen."

"Thank you for seeing us, Maureen. I'm Chief Inspector Whiteman and this is Inspector Williams. I know you must be busy so we'll try not to take too much of your time. We are trying to make contact with some of Stephen's work colleagues who may be able to tell us a little about him. Did you know him well?"

"Stephen's been on my ward for some eighteen months now," Maureen replied. "He was a very good nurse and a very likable person, but I only knew him through the work here."

"Did Stephen have friends here, any of the nurses or other members of staff?"

"The only close friend I'm aware of, Chief Inspector, is Andrew, Andrew Williams, but he's on holiday at the moment, due back tomorrow. I could get him to telephone you when he gets back."

"They were good friends?" asked Sheila."

"Yes they were. Andrew and Stephen lived together for a while up until about a year ago."

"And when Andrew moved out of Stephen's apartment was there any falling out, or any bad feeling?"

"No, not at all, not that I'm aware of anyway. On the contrary, they seemed to get on even better the last few months or so. Often went for drinks together after work here. I certainly wasn't aware of any problem or bad feeling."

"Did Stephen give the impression recently of having anything on his mind, any sign of him worrying about anything, or did you notice any change in him at all?"

"No, not that I'd noticed," replied Maureen.

"Is there anything else you can tell us, anything which might help?"

Maureen looked thoughtful for a moment then shook her head and looked at Sheila. "I'm sorry but there's absolutely nothing I can think of. Like everyone, I'm just totally shocked at what's happened. All of us here can hardly believe it."

Sheila handed Maureen her card. "OK, we'll get out of your way now, but I would appreciate you asking Andrew giving me a call when he gets back from holiday. Where's he gone by the way? Somewhere sunny I hope."

"Tunisia, I think he said he was going."

After another fifteen minutes or so of corridors and stairs, Sheila and Greg walked out of the main entrance and over to the car park. "OK, it looks like Stephen's friend, Andrew, was out of the country last night, but get Sergeant Ryan to check that out. Everything else is like a blank piece of paper at the moment," said Sheila. "There's absolutely nothing to go on apart from the way Stephen was murdered. But a hitman? What the hell is this all about?"

Chapter 5

The following morning Sheila was anxious to sort through the mountain of paperwork that had built up on her desk, a task that was not going to be made any easier by the new filing system she was attempting to get used to. She first needed to update Superintendent Davies about the Nurse Milligan shooting. Shouldn't take long, she thought, as she took the elevator to the fourth floor. Absolutely no progress on that at all. Sheila was quite taken aback with her superintendent's new office; very modern, and she thought the views across the city were really quite spectacular. At the far side of the office an ultra modern, black, glass-topped desk with shiny silver-coloured metal legs. Surrounding the walls stood several matching shiny black filing cabinets and side cupboards. Two black leather easy chairs and a matching black leather settee completed the furnishings, all of which gave the appearance of a top of the range, art deco style penthouse apartment. She couldn't help thinking all this made Superintendent Davies look somewhat out of place.

"How's everyone settling in to the new offices, Sheila? Any problems? DI Williams behaving himself I hope."

"Everyone seems to be settling in at the moment but, as you know, we've been a bit preoccupied the last twenty-four hours or so with the Nurse Milligan shooting."

"Yes, that was my next question. How's that progressing?"

"Very slowly at the moment, we've nothing concrete to go on yet. I'm hopeful that one of Stephen's friends, due back from holiday sometime today, may be able to tell us something. At the moment all we have is the shooting of a nurse by what looks as though it could be the work of a professional hitman. Forensic haven't come up with anything and, as for Nurse Milligan, so far all we've been able to discover is the fact he was gay, good at his job, well liked and respected, but not very good at handling his finances. I've got a meeting with everyone in about half an hour so I'm going to get Ryan, Finmore and DI Goode to start interviewing all of his colleagues. Someone's got to know something."

"OK, Sheila, I can see you've got your work cut out. I'll let you get on but keep me posted. Let me know as soon as there are any developments."

After collecting her notes from the main office Sheila made her way over to the incident room. "OK, everyone, let's see what we've managed to dig up on the murder of Nurse Milligan. And before we start I can confirm the results from forensic have produced nothing new. Greg and I briefly interviewed Margaret Entwhistle, the ward sister at the QE where Stephen was based. Nothing there either I'm afraid, just confirmation that Stephen was good at his job, reliable, hard-working and well liked. We know Stephen was gay and we shall be speaking with an Andrew Williams, also a nurse at the QE who was, we believe, a close friend of Stephen's. They shared the same apartment at Raddlebarn Court up to about nine months ago. Now, DI Goode, how did you get on with Stephen's parents? Anything interesting there?"

"Nice couple," he replied, "but nothing new. His parents were aware their son was gay. They had no problem with that at all; loved him even more. Stephen had two brothers and a sister, all older than him. I managed to speak with Graham, his eldest brother, and Laura, his sister. They both said pretty much the same things. Stephen was, according to them, a good, hard-working guy, loyal to his friends, with no enemies or problems that they were aware of. The only weakness he seemed to have was his inability to handle his finances. His father confirmed he'd bailed Stephen out a couple of times about two years ago, nothing big, a couple of grand so he told me, and nothing since."

Sheila looked across at DC Finmore. "You managed to get hold of the two tenants who were out yesterday did you, Constable?"

"Yes, both of them had the same opinion as all the other tenants. One of them, a Susan Pearce, did say she heard a car start up and drive off from the car park at the rear of the apartments at about one o'clock Monday morning. She didn't think anything of it and didn't bother to look so she couldn't tell me anything more. She heard nothing else that night."

"How was Miss. Pearce so sure of the time she'd heard this car start up?"

"She told me she'd just finished watching some late night movie. I did, in fact, check that out. There was a movie being shown that night which did finish at precisely one o'clock."

"Right, Constable, well now recheck all the CCTV footage near to Raddlebarn Court twenty minutes before and twenty minutes past one o'clock. Now we have an approximate time to go on you never know we might find something." Sheila with a look of some frustration turned to Sergeant Ryan. "And, Sergeant, have you found anything?"

"Gone through all Stephen's accounts and made all the usual checks, but nothing yet I'm afraid."

"OK, time for us to intensify our search a little. DI Goode, you and Sergeant Ryan go over to the QE. Speak with Margaret Entwhistle. I want you to go through the details of all the patients treated at the accident and emergency department for the last eighteen months since Stephen has been working there. I want details of anyone who's complained about the treatment received at the hospital. More especially, anyone Stephen was involved with treating who may have complained. Check with their GPs if necessary. I want to know everything that's happened there in the last eighteen months."

Greg looked over at Sheila. "You think it could be someone who's got a grudge against the hospital or against Stephen?"

"It's possible. We just look at everything at the moment. Sergeant Ryan, I want you to go over any complaint that's on record made by anyone about their treatment at the hospital. Go through everything and keep asking all the staff at the A & E department about anything they may know about Nurse Milligan. For the moment, everyone, that's all for now."

Greg looked at Sheila. It was obvious to him she was getting frustrated with things. A combination of moving to Birmingham Central, different offices, different routine and this case. "I think we could do with a drink, Sheila. How about we take a walk over to the Jeykll and Hyde? It's only five minutes away. We need to check it out sooner or later and now seems as good a time as any."

Sheila smiled. "OK, but you're paying this time."

That's more like it, thought Greg, as they walked over to the elevator. I'll break the news about forgetting my wallet when we get there.

The Jeykll and Hyde although recently refurbished remained every inch the typical Victorian public house. It had deep sculptured ceiling cornices and center roses. The walls, decorated with deeply embossed supaglypta paper, looked as though they'd been painted over a thousand times. The bar was busy with the usual lunchtime custom. Greg ordered two coffees and two ham sandwiches, and after emptying all the loose change from his pockets was just about able to pay the bill. Carrying the lunchtime sustenance on a tray Greg made his way over to the far side of the lounge where Sheila had found a reasonably quiet spot, a table next to one of the large stained glass windows.

"Here we are, Sheila. If I run out of cigarettes this afternoon you're going to have to bail me out. Forgot my wallet this morning and this lot's cleaned me out."

"No good coming to me, you need every reason to pack in that habit of yours. No good for you, you know that."

"Everyone knows that, Sheila. I will one day, but not yet." Greg looked at Sheila as he slowly stirred his coffee after emptying three envelopes of sugar into it. "This Milligan case, Sheila, it reminds me of the Dan Walters case about three years ago. Dan Walters was found stabbed to death at the front door of his house on the Kenilworth Road, Leamington Spa. It nearly drove DI Richards, who was heading the inquiry, insane searching for some sort of explanation. He looked at every possibility, and found absolutely nothing. Then, about six months into the enquirey, it was discovered to be a case of mistaken identity. Some drug dealers paid a couple of guys to bump off a Harry Poulson, but they got the wrong man. Poor old Dan Walters got a knife stuck in his back for absolutely no reason at all, and DI Richards nearly suffered a nervous breakdown."

"Come off it! You don't think the Milligan shooting is a case of mistaken identity any more than I do."

Greg, taking another sip of coffee, shrugged his shoulders. "No, not really, but you never know. What we both know, though, is you can't create leads that aren't there."

"They'll come in time, you'll see." Sheila's mobile bleeped. Picking it up from the table she read the message then looked at Greg. "That may be sooner than you think." Putting her mobile in her pocket Sheila

27

got up from the table. "Come on, Sergeant Ryan's discovered something which, according to this message, could be what we've been waiting for." Greg, hurriedly taking one last sip of coffee and picking up the remaining sandwich followed Sheila from the bar.

Chapter 6

Exiting the elevator Sheila and Greg walked across the main office to Sergeant Ryan's desk. "OK, Sergeant, got your text, what is it you've found for us?"

"I've come straight back here after speaking with a Colin Lawson, one of Nurse Milligan's colleagues at the QE. He told me something very interesting. Apparently, last August someone walked into the A & E department and collapsed. He was examined by one of the doctors, a Doctor Khan, who instructed Stephen Milligan and another nurse to get him into one of the side wards. He gave instructions for some tests to be carried out and said he'd take another look at him later. According to Colin they were overstretched as there'd been a pile-up on the M5 involving several cars, and a coach carrying fifty or so passengers. Anyway, about an hour later Stephen told him the patient who'd collapsed had discharged himself; just got up and walked out. Now when I spoke with Doctor Khan he remembered the incident. He told me he was surprised to say the least at what had happened. When he examined the man, in his assessment, there was no way he could have recovered in such a short space of time, certainly not enough to enable him to get up and walk out."

"Do you have a name for this man, Sergeant?"

"Thought you'd ask me that, Sheila. I think we do, and if we're right then this looks as though it's the opening we need. According to Nurse Lawson the name of the man was William Spears. He got the name from the patient's driving license and remembers the name because Spears is his wife's maiden name, and William is the name of his nephew. Anyway he gave me a brief description of the man. Mid-thirties, dark brown, almost black curly hair. I've run a check on him and if it's the same one, he's known to us. Not only us but the Belgian police who've been attempting to track him down over the past nine months in connection with one of the largest diamond robberies ever which took place at Brussels Airport last June. I'm waiting for more information on that but I thought I'd bring you up to date straight away. Oh, and by the way, we've had a call from Andrew Williams, you know, Stephen Milligan's friend. He's back from holiday and has just heard the news about Stephen from Margaret Entwhistle, the ward sister at A & E. He sounded in a right panic, really upset. I said you'd want to speak with him and I'd give him a call later to arrange that."

"OK, Sergeant, well done. Telephone Andrew Williams and tell him I'd like to call over and see him straight away. Is he at home or at the hospital?"

"At home all day, so he told me." Sergeant Ryan wrote down the address and telephone number and handed the note to Sheila.

"Right, Sergeant, get in touch with the Belgian police. I think a word with whoever's in charge of investigating this diamond robbery you've just mentioned might be able to tell us something but, before that, get a definite identification of this William Spears from Nurse Harper. Right, Greg, let's go. Andrew Williams first, then we'll have a word with Doctor Khan."

Andrew Williams had purchased some nine months previously a two-bedroom Victorian terraced property in Cotteridge, just a few miles from Stephen Milligan's apartment. Unlike his friend, Stephen, who was quite happy to remain in rented accommodation, Andrew had been far more ambitious. He'd always wanted to secure a foothold on the property ladder. Andrew, having only moved into 14 Carters Close less than a year ago, had already begun, thought Sheila, to put his mark on his investment. Two enormous stone flowerpots sat each side of what was obviously a newly painted front door. The very latest designer chrome fittings – door handle, bell, letterbox, and doorknocker – all glistened in the sunlight. The door opened immediately as Sheila pressed the designer bell. "You must be the police? Come in won't you. Excuse the mess. I've only got back from holiday a couple of hours ago. I haven't been to the supermarket yet so, I'm sorry I can't even offer you a cup of tea." There was no hallway to number fourteen. The front door led straight into the front reception room which, from the smell of paint, like the front door, had been given a make-over.

"Andrew Williams?" began Sheila.

"Yes, that's me."

"Andrew, I'm DCI Whiteman and this is DI Williams."

"Yes, I had a call from one of your officers to say you were on your way over." Andrew, a slim, mid-thirties character, thought Sheila, looked nervous, and from the look in his eyes obviously very upset. Not allowing Sheila the opportunity to speak Andrew nervously went on. "What happened to Stephen? I just can't believe it. Maureen texted me at the airport in Tunisia just before I boarded my flight. She told me Stephen had been murdered. I telephoned her as soon I got back here. She said Stephen had been shot and I was to telephone you straight away. I can't believe it. What on earth is going on?" Andrew took a cigarette from the packet on the side table and shakily held the lighter to ignite the desperately needed weed. Sheila was quick to grab the opportunity to speak.

"Well, that's what we wanted to talk to you about, Andrew. Yes, I'm sorry to have to tell you Stephen was found dead at his apartment last Monday morning. What can you tell us about him?"

Andrew, who was still pacing up and down, turned to Sheila. "Please sit down both of you. You must think I'm so rude. It's just all been such a shock." Sheila and Greg sat down on the sofa, Andrew on the edge of the armchair opposite them. "I've known Stephen for a number of years, Inspector. We got on really well. He was a lovely man, a good nurse, hard-working and fun to be with."

"You lived with Stephen for a while I understand?"

"Yes, at his apartment at Raddlebarn Court up until a few months ago before I bought this place. I didn't want to be renting all my life."

"You and Stephen didn't consider buying a property together then?"

"We talked about it, Inspector, on more than one occasion but..." Andrew hesitated, "...Stephen wasn't really that interested. All he wanted was a good time, new clothes, holidays, new car, going out all the time, all those things, so we tended to go our separate ways a little over the past year."

"What can you tell me about Stephen's friends? Did he have any enemies you know of? Do you know of anyone who'd want to harm him?"

"He was liked by everybody," said Andrew. "There's absolutely no one I could describe as not taking to him. He had no enemies at all, the very thought someone has killed him is…well, it's just unbelievable."

It was obvious to Sheila she would need to take her time with Andrew. His thoughts and emotions were all over the place. "Can you tell me, Andrew, anything about a man who came into the A & E ward you and Stephen were working on last year and collapsed? We understand he simply checked out again after about an hour without any apparent reason."

Sheila sensed she'd hit a nerve. Andrew looked awkward. "We have patients behaving oddly all the time. It's not unusual, Inspector. A lot of people suddenly get an attack of nerves and walk out."

"The person I'm referring to, Andrew, checked into the hospital on Saturday evening, the 21st of June last year. You may remember that night. There had been a pile-up on the M5 apparently, involving several cars and a coach. Nurse Lawson and Doctor Khan have both confirmed how busy you all were that evening."

Andrew lit another cigarette. "I vaguely remember something about a patient checking himself out that night but, as you're already aware, we were extremely busy and I really can't recall that much about it."

Sheila showed Andrew her mobile with the picture of William Spears that Sergeant Ryan had put on her phone. "Was this the man who collapsed that night, Andrew?"

Andrew glanced at the picture on Sheila's mobile. Even the ten days of Tunisian sunshine couldn't hide the paleness rushing to his face." It could be, but I really couldn't be absolutely sure."

"All right, Andrew, we'll get out of your way for now and let you get on with your unpacking. We'll probably want to speak to you again, so if you can think of anything which may be of help please let me know."

As they drove off Greg turned to Sheila. "You left that one a bit short, Sheila."

"Yes, he's hiding something," said Sheila, "and before we begin to delve further I'd like to find out a bit more about this William Spears first, so we'll make a start with Doctor Khan."

The receptionist at the QE put a call out for Doctor Khan and asked Sheila and Greg to take a seat. Five minutes later, Doctor Khan walked over to them.

"Doctor Khan, thank you for seeing us."

"Not a problem, Chief Inspector, please follow me, we can use the office over here by reception." As Doctor Khan walked across the reception hall, Sheila felt relieved they were not about to start trekking along what seemed at their last visit to be endless miles of corridors and stairways. They followed Doctor Khan into a small office with four chairs, a table and several filing cabinets. "Now, Chief Inspector, how can I help you? I take it this is to do with the shooting of Nurse Milligan the other day?"

"It is, Doctor. What can you tell us about him?"

"He was a good nurse, a very likable person, hard-working and reliable. Apart from that I really don't know what I can tell you about him."

"You don't know of anyone who'd want to hurt him, anyone he'd fallen out with recently?"

Doctor Khan shrugged his shoulders. "I didn't know Stephen personally at all. I can only tell you what I know from his work here, and what everyone else is saying. It's been a shock to all of us, Inspector."

"Last year, Saturday the 21st of June to be precise, a patient you examined here that evening apparently checked himself out before you could finish your examination of him. We understand you were somewhat surprised at that. Can you tell us anything more about that?"

"Well, if it's the person I assume you're referring to, the only thing I can say is I was amazed he'd recovered sufficiently to have managed to walk anywhere. My initial examination suggested he was suffering from a virus or some other infection. I gave instructions for Nurse Milligan to arrange a bed for him in one of the side wards and to carry out some tests whilst I continued attending to the other patients we had that evening."

"Yes, I'd heard it was a busy night for you."

"Every night is busy, Chief Inspector, but that evening even more so due to an accident on the M5."

Sheila showed the photograph of William Spears on her mobile. "Is this the patient you saw, Doctor Khan?"

Glancing at Sheila's mobile, Doctor Khan nodded. "Yes, that looks like him, Chief Inspector."

"You say after you'd examined him you thought he was suffering from a virus or an infection of some kind. Can you be more specific?"

"Not really, Inspector, I remember he had a couple of burn marks on his hands and on his right arm which could have been a reaction to a virus infection. It was also possible it had been caused by the patient coming into contact with some acidic substance. However, what I do remember is that he was very weak, and unconscious. As I've just told you I was surprised to say the least when I was informed he'd checked himself out less than an hour after I'd seen him. But apparently he did and that is, I'm afraid, all I remember."

"Were any notes made which you could refer to?"

"There were, but for some reason they seemed to have gone missing. I asked both Nurse Milligan and Nurse Williams if they knew what had happened to them but they had no idea." Doctor Khan's bleeper sounded. "Chief Inspector, you'll have to excuse me, I have an emergency."

Standing up, Sheila shook hands with Doctor Khan. "If you could give some thought as to what may have caused William Spears to fall ill I would be extremely grateful. It could be helpful to our enquiry."

Doctor Khan shook his head. Half smiling he looked at Sheila. "I will give it some thought, Chief Inspector, but you must understand I saw this patient for less than fifteen minutes over twelve months ago. Without the results from any of the tests I'd carried out, my opinion would be nothing more than a wild guess."

As Greg was driving back to Birmingham Sheila, looking out of the passenger window, was in deep thought. "You know, a couple of hours ago we were looking at a blank piece of paper with regards to the shooting of Stephen Milligan. Now we have someone Stephen attended to last year who rather strangely goes missing, and not only that but someone who's wanted for questioning by the Belgian police in connection with that diamond robbery at Brussels Airport. We just may be on to something." Looking over at Sheila, Greg thought it was either that or wishful thinking." As soon as we get back, Greg, get everyone together in the incident room."

Chapter 7

At Birmingham Central, Sergeant Ryan had more news for Sheila. Andrew Williams was waiting for her. "Called in about half an hour ago. I put him in interview room four downstairs."

"OK, Sergeant. Now I want you and DI Goode to watch and take note. I'll want your thoughts later. Greg, you sit in with me." Andrew seems a little more composed, thought Sheila, as she and Greg entered the interview room. "Andrew, I appreciate you calling to see us."

"Thank you, Chief Inspector. I just want to clarify a few things with you, that's all. It's about the man who came into A & E last year, you know, the one you showed me the photograph of earlier."

"OK, Andrew, what can you tell us about him?"

"Well, I remember now. He came into A & E last June as you know, and then suddenly collapsed. Stephen and Colin attended to him and then Doctor Khan examined him. He gave instructions for him to be put in one of the side wards and for some tests to be carried out. About an hour later Stephen told me the patient who'd collapsed had telephoned someone to pick him up, and had just checked himself out. Now I didn't say anything at the time, but I saw Stephen pushing someone out of the main entrance in a wheelchair. When I asked him about that he said he was simply helping one of the other patients to a car which was waiting outside."

"Did you see who it was in the wheelchair, Andrew?"

"No, I only saw Stephen pushing the chair from behind. I couldn't see who was in the chair, but later, in fact several weeks later, Stephen told me it was William Spears. I knew all along he was hiding something. Now I don't know whether this will be of any help to you but I also remember seeing Stephen talking to a couple of guys about twenty minutes before I saw him pushing the wheelchair out of the main entrance. When I asked him who they were he seemed evasive, just said he couldn't remember. I've been concerned about all this for a long time because if Stephen had helped an unconscious patient out of the hospital then I should have reported it, or made Stephen report the incident. The simple fact is I really wasn't sure what happened except it was obvious to me Stephen was hiding something. That was one of the things I was worried about when you came to see me this morning."

"OK, Andrew, you made the right decision to come and tell us what you know. Firstly, are you sure the man who collapsed that night was the same man in the picture I showed you this morning?"

"Yes, it was the same person, no doubt about that."

"Where were you, Andrew, when this man collapsed?"

"I was in reception collecting some notes from one of the nurses."

"And you saw the man in the photograph I showed you this morning collapse?" asked Sheila.

"Yes, that's right."

"What did you do?"

"I was about to go over to him when Stephen and Colin walked over to attend to him."

"About how far away were you?"

"Not far, about ten meters or so," Andrew replied. "I was at the main desk collecting some notes for one of the doctors, and was about to take them over to him."

"Did you go over to the man you saw collapse?"

"Yes, for a moment. Stephen and Colin had the situation in hand so I got on with what I was doing. We were extremely busy that night due to the accident on the M5 I told you about this morning."

Sheila continued, "And the people you mentioned you saw Stephen talking to earlier, had you seen either of those people before?"

"No, never. I've no idea who they were. They may just have been relatives of one of the patients, or asking the way to one of the wards or something. I don't really know."

"But you remembered them, Andrew, so what was it that made you remember them?"

"They just looked out of place. There wasn't anything specific I can remember about them really." Andrew hesitated for a moment then looked at Sheila. "Don't take this the wrong way, Chief Inspector, but they somehow looked like one of your lot, very official looking, you know."

"OK, Andrew, we can come back to that later. Were you aware that Stephen had come into rather a lot of money last year?"

"Yes, he didn't tell me anything about it, not straight away anyway. I only found out by accident. I happened to see his building society passbook which he'd left on the bedside cabinet and I picked it up by mistake. I thought it was mine. I have an account with the Coventry Building Society as well. When I found it, it explained a lot to me. You see, Stephen seemed to have changed quite a lot since we'd been living together. I knew he'd got some money from somewhere. We went on two holidays – one to Spain, one to Tunisia. I told him we couldn't afford it but he just said he'd pay and to stop worrying. Then he bought a new car, well not a new one, an MGB roadster, quite a classic actually. He'd been going on about getting one for ages. Twelve grand he paid for it, and no finance. I was there when he handed over the cash. So it didn't take much to realize he'd come into some money from somewhere or other."

"Did you ask him about that?"

"Yes, he just said he'd had a stroke of luck on the horses. I knew that wasn't true. Stephen had never gambled in his life, and as for horse racing he didn't know one end of a horse from the other."

"Did Stephen share any of the money he'd said he'd won? Did he help with your deposit for the purchase of your house at Carters Close?"

"Yes, he did actually. Five grand, which I offered to pay him back over a period of time, but he refused. Said he could get some more when he needed it."

"Did he elaborate at all on that? Did he tell you where he was going to get the money from?"

"No, Chief Inspector, he didn't. He was always a very private person anyway, always kept things to himself. Everything I've told you I only found out by chance."

"OK, Andrew, I'll probably want to speak to you again but we'll leave things there for the moment." Greg showed Andrew to the reception area then he and Sheila took the elevator to the main office. "Get everyone together, Greg. We need to update everyone and decide where we go from here."

Ten minutes later everyone had assembled in the incident room and Sheila began to go over the progress so far. "OK, everyone, we now believe that a William Spears, who incidentally is known to both ourselves and the Belgian police, checked himself into the A & E ward at the Queen Elizabeth on the 21st of June last year then suddenly collapsed. He was attended by Stephen Milligan, another nurse Colin Lawson and a Doctor Khan. Instructions were given by Doctor Khan to arrange a bed for William Spears in one of the side wards, and for some tests to be carried out. About an hour later, according to what Stephen Milligan told his colleague Andrew Williams, William Spears had telephoned a friend to collect him from the hospital and checked himself out. Now I've spoken to both Doctor Khan and Nurse Lawson who have expressed their surprise at how William Spears recovered sufficiently enough in such a short space of time to be able to do that. I interviewed Andrew Williams a few moments ago and he told me that Stephen Milligan helped William Spears out of the hospital, apparently in a wheelchair. He also told me that Stephen Milligan told him he was able to get his hands on some cash and suggested this would be from the same source as the £25,000 he paid into his building society account last year. Andrew also mentioned that he saw Stephen Milligan talking to two men in the reception area at A & E just before he'd apparently helped William Spears check out." Sheila, with a wry smile, continued, "He remembers these men because he thought they looked like 'one of our lot', as he put it. Now, moving on, we've also discovered the Belgian police have been looking for William Spears in connection with a diamond robbery which took place at Brussels Airport last June. Diamonds and gold worth £100m were stolen. I'm told it was one of the biggest robberies ever. I'm waiting for more details which I should have in the morning, so I'll be able to update you tomorrow."

DI Goode looked over at Sheila. "The Brussels Airport diamond robbery, Sheila? I remember it. It was one of the biggest heists ever. There were £90m of uncut diamonds apparently, and about £10m in gold bullion. So if William Spears was involved in that, and was being tracked by the Belgian police, maybe his counterparts decided to get him out of the way. He checks himself into A & E with some problem or other then, being followed by members of his gang, they decide to get him away from the hospital, and if that's so never to be seen again probably. Then Stephen Milligan is paid for his help in getting William Spears out of hospital, but when he goes back for some more money they eliminate him as well."

Sheila could see the logic in that theory. "It's possible, Inspector, but at the moment it's just that, a possibility, so in the morning I want you and Constable Finmore to interview everyone who was on duty that night at the A & E ward. See if you can find anyone who might have seen the people Stephen Milligan was talking to just before William Spears checked out, or anything else they may remember. And check if there's any CCTV footage. I doubt there'll be any anything as far back as last June but you never know. Right, that's all for now but I want you all back here tomorrow at one o'clock. I should have the details on the diamond robbery William Spears was suspected of being involved in. Sheila turned to Greg. "Right, I'm thirsty, John's not back until Friday and I need some intelligent feedback on all this so, no arguments, I'll see you at mine in an hour."

Chapter 8

Greg was quite used to the out of hours conferences Sheila insisted on having. The bottles of wine she always held in stock on the rack in her kitchen being the plus side to these informal discussions. Greg was still renting Sheila's old apartment at Wake Green Road which was, rather conveniently, situated just a five minute walk from 'Ash Views', Salisbury Road, the house Sheila shared with her partner John Scarsbrook QC. Rain, hail or shine, Greg always walked the half mile or so to John and Sheila's house. It solved the drink drive problems an inspector of Her Majesty's constabulary could not afford to ignore. Sheila had just put the Chinese takeaway she'd bought on her way home for her and Greg in the warming oven as the doorbell rang. "Right, Greg, you know where the wine is. Get a bottle and a couple of glasses and I'll sort the takeaway out." Settling themselves in the lounge Greg poured two glasses of wine as Sheila placed the cartons of prawns, rice and chips on the coffee table. "What did you make of Andrew Williams, Greg?"

"I'm not completely convinced by his interpretation of events. Everything he told us was from a spectator's point of view and, unless I'm mistaken, it seemed his interpretation of events had been thought through and well rehearsed if you ask me."

"I had the same impression. You think he was more involved than he's letting on?"

"Well…just a guess, Sheila."

"OK, we'll have another word with him in the next few days. Meanwhile, see what Ryan and Goode think in the morning. Get them to take a good look at the recording. If he was more involved than he's letting on then it's possible he could be in danger of being bumped off as well."

Greg pouring himself another glass of red passed the bottle to Sheila. "At the moment we're working on the possibility that Billy Spears was involved in that diamond robbery at Brussels Airport last year, and one of the gang got Stephen Milligan to help get him out of hospital. They pay him £25,000 for his help and then, when he goes back for more money, they bump him off. But there are a couple of things there that don't quite gel. Firstly, why did they want him out of hospital so desperately in the first place? Secondly, if that is what happened, how was it Stephen Milligan was able to get back in touch with them again? You wouldn't expect them to leave their calling card with Stephen, would you?"

"No you wouldn't. The first thing we need to do is get the details of that investigation the Brussels police are working on, and see exactly what they've got on Billy Spears." Sheila's mobile rang. Greg could tell from the expression on her face the call was important. "OK, see you when you get there, Sergeant." Sheila put the mobile back on the side table. Deep in thought, she looked at Greg. "You're not going to believe this. Sergeant Ryan has just been updated about the investigation into that diamond robbery last year. Now guess who Inspector Claes of the Brussels Federal Police reckon masterminded it. None other than Franz Zimmerman, and who do you think has been assisting him in his investigation the last few months? Our old friend DI Partridge from the Met."

Greg, always quick to respond went into the kitchen and collected two more bottles from the wine rack. Returning to the lounge he placed the bottles on the coffee table. "My guess is we'll need a few more of these, Sheila, before this investigation is over. So this Inspector from Belgium, whatever his name is, believes Franz Zimmerman was the brains behind the robbery? But the day the robbery took place, Raena McCory was about to run a sword through him and run off with that painting by Degas."

Just as Sheila was about to elaborate the doorbell rang. "That'll be Ryan now." She turned to Greg as she went to answer the door, "Go easy on the wine."

Sergeant Ryan came into the lounge with a folder of papers under his arm. "Hi, Greg, found the wine then?"

"He has, and before it's all gone I'll get you a glass." Sheila came back from the kitchen and handed her sergeant a glass. "Right, pour yourself a glass while there's still some left. Now, let's have a look at what you've managed to dig up for us." Sheila opened the folder Ryan had bought with him as her sergeant, taking a gulp from his glass of red, placed the glass on the coffee table and began.

"I managed to get an update on the investigation into that diamond robbery last year. It's being headed by a Chief Inspector Michiel Claes of the Belgium Federal Police who, incidentally, is over here now in London working with DCI Partridge who I spoke with earlier. Oh, and by the way, he and Inspector Claes want to come over to Birmingham for an update on the Milligan shooting. Apparently, so Inspector Partridge informs me, about a month into the investigation the Belgian police received an anonymous tip-off that the robbery had been planned by Franz Zimmerman, and gave the names of two of the perpetrators, William Spears and a George McCann. Now, when they ran a check on Spears and McCann they discovered they both had records, and Spears's fingerprints were found on one of the cases taken from the aircraft. Not the cases containing the diamonds but one of the cases holding the gold which was left about a mile away from where the vehicles used in the raid had been abandoned. Now, straight after the robbery both William Spears and George McCann seemed to disappear. According to DI Partridge, when they visited McCann's last known address in Dudley, his landlady, a Mrs. Elson, said she hadn't seen him since last June. She couldn't recall the precise date, but what she did remember was he wasn't well, obviously caught some bug or something and, this is the interesting bit, two guys came round late one night and helped McCann into their car and drove off. They told Mrs. Elson, the landlady, that they were taking him to hospital to get him checked out. And that was the last time she saw him."

"Bit of a coincidence don't you think?" said Sheila, as she poured herself another glass of wine. "Both Spears and McCann are suddenly taken ill and now they seem to have disappeared altogether. We need to update our investigation here with this Inspector Claes from Belgium and DI Partridge. You say DI Partridge and Inspector Claes are coming to Birmingham tomorrow?"

"Yes, they asked me to confirm a time we can all get together."

"That's fine by me," said Sheila, "However, I'm not going to be messed around and left in the dark again as happened with the Zimmerman fiasco."

Chapter 9

Ronnie White had been very patient. It was almost sixteen months since he'd organized and taken part in what had gone down as one of the largest robberies of all time. That accolade had in some ways helped him to keep calm and take his time in planning to track down the £90m worth of uncut diamonds which had gone missing shortly after he and his team had returned home from Brussels. Ronnie's girlfriend, Debra, had even compiled a scrapbook on the heist, painstakingly cutting out all the national reports on the robbery. She'd made four DVDs of the news reports from all the main TV channels including a *Panorama* investigation broadcast just over a month previously. The story had been big news, and the word had spread quickly through the underworld that Ronnie White was the mastermind and the main operator behind the heist. He had become, within the criminal fraternity, an even bigger celebrity than any of his predecessors making the Kray twins, the Richardson brothers and others pale into insignificance by this achievement. Ronnie White was definitely the new king of the underworld. All this made him feel good, but his task now was to find out what happened to the diamonds just three days after he and his gang had returned to England. Ronnie's partner in the heist, Franz Zimmerman, who had in fact been the real brains behind the robbery, had been found murdered the same day Ronnie and his team carried out the heist at Brussels Airport. He'd been found dead with a replica of a sword used in the Battle of Hastings stuck through his chest pinning him to the back of the chair he'd been sitting in at the lounge of his home at Broom Hall. Raena McCory, a twenty-eight-year-old prostitute, had been charged with his murder and the theft of a painting by the French artist, Edgar Degas, a painting reportedly worth in the region of £2m. Raena McCory, however, was found not guilty. The murder of Franz Zimmerman and the ensuing trial of Raena McCory was as big a story as the diamond heist in Belgium, albeit for totally different reasons. During the trial of Raena McCory it was discovered that Franz Zimmerman was one of the originators and financiers of an organization calling itself the Knights Templar, an organization referred to by the mass murderer Anders Behring Breivik at his trial at the Oslo District Court in Norway. The Knights Templar organization, a far right fascist group who'd been guilty of murdering dozens of immigrant workers who'd moved to the UK at the end of the Second World War, and British intelligence were still busy attempting to keep under wraps the names of some of their more prominent members.

Ronnie was sitting in the drawing room of the house in the Cotswold village of Moreton-in-Marsh which he and his girlfriend Debra Williams had moved to just over eighteen months previously. Ronnie was going over and over what might have happened, just as he had done every day since last June. The 15th of June 2012 was when Ronnie and his gang had returned to England with their prize, £90m of uncut diamonds. The plan, agreed with Franz Zimmerman, was to hide the diamonds until things had cooled down. Twelve months, perhaps a little longer, then their contact in Amsterdam would begin to carry out the process of cutting the diamonds and selling them over a period of time, two or three years maybe. The initial plan was to hide the diamonds at Zimmerman's residence, Broom Hall. Ronnie had agreed he'd take the diamonds over there and meet up with Franz Zimmerman who'd show him where they'd be kept. Then, just before boarding the flight back home from Brussels, Ronnie received a text from his girlfriend Debra Williams. The police were at their house with a search warrant, and a warrant for his arrest. Ronnie was aware the visit from the police had nothing to do with the robbery he and his gang had just successfully completed. He knew that for sure. Had they the slightest suspicion he'd been involved in the robbery at Brussels Airport he would have been arrested before his flight back home. Besides, Ronnie had a good idea what they wanted. He was not, however, about to return home with £90m of uncut diamonds in the boot of his car. Unaware Zimmerman had been stabbed to death just a few hours earlier he hurriedly arranged for George and William to deliver the cartons to Broom Hall. Arriving back home Ronnie was arrested for a totally unrelated matter. His parole was cancelled and he was promptly returned to Wormwood Scrubs. Now, less than twelve months later, he was a free man again and determined to find out what had happened to the diamonds. Alan Richards, who Ronnie regarded as the senior member of his gang, was calling to see him to go over ideas of how they were going to begin their search. Ronnie lit a cigarette and looked at his watch. Another ten minutes, he thought, and he'll be here. Debra walked into the lounge in the shortest of skirts. It had just turned eleven o'clock, but she looked like she was dressed for a night on the town. "How ya feeling, Ron, glad to be home with all your creature comforts? Including me?" she giggled.

"I am, Deb, you know that. Alan's due here in a minute. We need to talk about the sparklers, and where they might be hidden."

"Well just don't get pushing your luck with things. I hate it when you're not here."

"I'm not exactly over the moon with the accommodation I'm provided with at the Scrubs either, Deb. Don't worry, there'll be no more slip-ups."

"I think your lad, Alan, is here, Ron," said Debra peering out of the window. "I'll go and let him in shall I?"

"Yer show him in, Deb, and bring a few cans from the fridge would you, love."

Debra showed Alan Richards into the drawing room. "I'll get the drinks, Ron," said Debra as she slipped out of the room.

"How are you, Ronnie? Good to see you back home again. How's everyone at B wing?"

Ronnie smiled. "All a bunch of fucking wimps these days. Don't know what the world's coming to. Right, Alan, the diamonds. We need to find them." Ronnie, staring out of the window overlooking the half acre of gardens, turned to Alan. "And find them we will, if it's the last thing I do."

Debra came in with the cans of lager and placed them on the sideboard. "I'll leave you two to talk business. I'm in the dining room if you want me, Ron." Debra closed the door behind her as Alan offered Ronnie a cigarette. After lighting up the weeds Alan helped himself to one of the cans from the sideboard, opened it, took a gulp and sat down. Ronnie, taking another drag from his cigarette looked straight at him.

"OK, Alan, the diamonds. Any ideas?"

"You mean apart from Billy and George doing a runner with them?"

"They didn't do a runner with them," retorted Ronnie. "I know that. They'd neither the balls nor the brains to organize anything like that. And Franz Zimmerman had nothing to do with it either as he, as we're all aware, was well and truly dead before we arrived back home. However, he would have known where Billy and George were to hide them. He said he'd have someone meet us when we got to Broom Hall and they'd show us exactly where they were to be hidden."

"So where the fuck do we go from here, Ron, if Billy and George didn't nick them, and Zimmerman was busy stoking the fires down below? Where the hell are they hidden?"

"That's what we're going to find out, and I think I know someone who may be able to help us." Ronnie stubbed out his cigarette in the ashtray on the coffee table and leant back in his chair. "Raena McCory. I think it's time we called on her expertize."

Alan, halfway through taking another swig from his can of lager, spluttered. After finishing coughing he looked at Ronnie in amazement. "Raena McCory? What, that anorexic-looking lesbian hooker? Come off it, Ron, what use could she be? Besides, she's no longer at Broom Hall, and apart from all that there are still more coppers going over that place than at the Met, not counting all the spooks from MI5 or wherever they hang out. The Hall, what's left of it, and the entire estate is still completely sealed off. We've no chance of finding anything there and I can't see how the hell you think Miss. McCory could help."

Ronnie, taking no notice of Alan's objections, was still thinking through his ideas. Taking a deep breath he looked at Alan. "Raena McCory is not your usual kind of girl, Alan. Last year she gets into Broom Hall, gives the place the once over with those bugging devices of hers then sticks a socking great sword through Zimmerman and nicks one of his paintings. When charged she goes to court, virtually tells everyone to fuck off, gets a not guilty verdict and walks free, and with a painting worth £2m!" Ronnie with a broad grin looked at Alan again. "I don't care what you say about her, that's my kind of girl. I'll make contact with her, maybe invite her for a meal with you, me and Deb. I'll make it all very professional and discuss the idea with her, an idea

47

which could earn her a lot of money. If what I've heard about our Miss. McCory is correct an offer of a few million pound finders fee, tax free, will be like music to her ears."

"I don't doubt that, Ron, but I still can't think how she can be any help."

Ronnie smiled, "That's because you don't know her. Take it from me she's a very talented young lady, and holds a lot of information in that pretty head of hers about all the goings on at Broom Hall and Zimmerman's empire. She lives in Worcester somewhere. It won't be difficult to find her. I'll make contact and put the idea to her."

Chapter 10

The telephone was ringing at Raena's penthouse apartment just as she was exiting the elevator on the fourth floor of Worcester House. Raena, expecting a call from one of her clients, hurriedly turned the key to the front door and, dropping her case in the hallway, walked into the lounge and picked up the receiver. She answered, as always, with a simple, "Hello."

"Raena, it's Christine, can I stop over at yours tonight?" Christine Henderson, was a good friend of Raena's. She worked in the same 'entertainment' business and had even helped Raena create an alibi for the night Franz Zimmerman was murdered.

"Christine, how are you, love? Course you can stay over if you want to. You're lucky to catch me. I've only just this minute got back from visiting my gran in Germany. Where are you, and what time do you want to call round?"

"I'm on the train from Paddington. I should be at Snow Hill Station in about half an hour."

"Oh yes, and what have you been up to in London? Hope you're not trying to nick my clients at Canary Wharf!"

"No such luck, Raena. I've been to one of Kate's introductions. Works at MI5 apparently, or so I've been told."

"You mean to tell me you've been down London shagging James Bond without inviting me?"

Christine laughed. "He wasn't James Bond, Raena, I can assure you of that, and a right weirdo. You wouldn't have liked him...although thinking about it you'd have probably had the time of your life."

"Thank you, Christine, you did say you wanted to stay over tonight didn't you?"

"I did, and thanks, Raena. See you in about an hour."

"OK, Chris, no rush. I'm here all night." Raena loved her gran dearly and made a point of visiting her every four to six weeks at her cottage in Fritzlar, Germany, but was always glad when she got back home. Her luxuriously appointed penthouse apartment had top of the range designer furniture, a sixty-five inch plasma TV and luxurious deep pile carpets, all of which Raena had worked hard for. Her expertize in the profession she'd chosen not only thrilled her but generated a very sizeable income, almost half of which had been completely tax free. Raena's expertize and understanding of the business world, coupled with her wide understanding of the money markets, were all part of her very formidable repertoire.

This, the first of Raena's professions, ran well with her second occupation as a high-class hooker. Her list of clients looked like something out of who's who. Bankers, politicians, sports personalities from all corners of the world would pay handsomely for her company and expertize in the art of pushing their exploration of sexual experiences to new heights. Raena was one of the few of her profession who genuinely enjoyed her work, both with her male and female clients. As with all her activities, Raena coupled her expertize both in and out of the bedroom with an assortment of very sophisticated bugging devices which gave her the inside information she used from time to time in her business activities. She was, as one of the directors of the International Monetary Fund once described her, a creation of the gods holding the secret of the Midas touch.

Raena came out of the lounge stripping naked as she walked down the hallway to the bathroom. Standing in the shower she indulged in the feeling of hot water running over her turning the gel she massaged into her slim frame into a creation of foam which, slowly, as if caressing every contour of her body, slid over her. After enjoying these few moments of relaxation and self-indulgence Raena dried herself, slipped on a short towel tunic and walked back into the lounge. Pouring herself a glass of wine she lit a cigarette and relaxed on the sofa. She had a busy week ahead. Thursday, in her escorting role, she was accompanying one of the traders at HSBC, Canary Wharf, to New York for a meeting with administrators who'd been called in by the directors of a large chain of newsagents and bookshops. The visit there, which was to last until Saturday, would earn Raena around £6,000, and would give her the insight into the organization she'd need when advising one of her Manchester clients on whether to invest in the restructuring of the enterprise. Successful or otherwise, her fee for that part of the exercise would bring in another £6,000. Then, she thought to herself, Sunday and Monday I'll have a break. With her magical green eyes Raena looked up at the ceiling and ran her fingers through her short blond hair. She was looking forward to catching up with her friend, Christine. Maybe a meal out tonight, she thought, at her favorite restaurant in Worcester, the Manderin.

About to pour herself another glass of wine Raena's thoughts were interrupted by the buzz of the intercom. Strange, she thought, can't be Christine, she only telephoned fifteen minutes ago. The camera image showed a well-dressed, elderly man with greying hair. No idea who that is, thought Raena. She was tempted to ignore it and go back to pouring her wine, however, curiosity won the moment. Pressing the response button Raena leant forward slightly. "Yes, can I help you?"

"Is that Raena McCory?"

"How can I help you?"

"Miss. McCory, my name's Ronnie, Ronnie White. We haven't met before but I wondered if I might have a quick word with you about a business proposition I'd like to discuss with you. If it's not convenient right now can we perhaps arrange a time to meet up?"

Raena was hesitant. She didn't know the man standing at the entrance of the apartment block, she'd never seen him before and was about to say it was not convenient, but again her curiosity got the better of her. Never one to turn away from any possible opportunity Raena pressed the entrance button. "I can give you a couple of minutes, but that's all. I'm on the fourth floor." Raena hearing the sound of the elevator doors opening walked out of her apartment to the center landing to meet her mystery guest. Exiting the elevator, the very attractive, thought Raena, mystery guest walked over to where she was standing.

"Miss. McCory, thanks for seeing me."

Satisfying herself the guy seemed OK, Raena invited him into her apartment. They walked through to the lounge. Raena, picking up a glass from the side cabinet, turned to her guest. "Ronnie, you say your name is? Well, would you like a drink, Ronnie?"

"That would be nice, thanks." Ronnie took a seat in the enormous armchair opposite Raena who sat down on the settee.

"OK, how can I help you? You say you have some business you wish to discuss?"

"Yes, that's right. I'll get straight to the point, Raena. You worked with Franz Zimmerman for a while at his home at Broom Hall, and I believe you may be able to help me locate some items I left with him for safe keeping."

Raena was quickly losing interest. "And what makes you think I can be of any help?"

"Well you worked with Zimmerman for over twelve months. You know all about him, his business interests and his contacts."

Raena had now completely lost interest in her mystery guest's proposition as he'd described it. Getting up from the settee Raena had decided to end the discussion. "I'm not being rude but anything to do with the late Franz Zimmerman is of no interest to me. You're wasting your time. I'm sorry if you've had a wasted journey."

Ronnie beamed a smile at Raena. "All I'm after, Raena, are some items left at Broom Hall, or close by, the day after Franz Zimmerman was murdered. If you can help us find them then there's a reward." Raena still not interested was about to show her guest from her apartment when the amount of the reward on offer was mentioned. "The reward is £2m, Raena, and all you have to do is point me in the right direction."

"Did you say £2m? Is this some sort of joke?" Raena's mind was working overtime as she sat back on the settee. "What exactly is it you're looking for at Broom Hall? You know the place was all but destroyed in the fire they had there, and apart from that it's still very much a crime scene. You won't get near the place without every copper and secret service agent hanging about out there knowing."

"I am aware of the difficulties, Raena, which is why, I believe we could benefit from your expertize. Now, before we go any further, it's probably a good idea we clear the air. Come clean so to speak. When you were busy running a sword through Franz Zimmerman and running off with one of his paintings, I and my associates were also quite busy nicking £90m of uncut diamonds from an aircraft at Brussels Airport."

Suddenly, Raena twigged. "Of course! You're the Ronnie White it's rumored carried out the great diamond robbery as it's called. Well I'm pleased to meet you, Ronnie, but, I'm sorry, I'm really not about to get myself involved in anything to do with that. No disrespect and, believe me, our chat here this evening will go no further, but I think all this is way out of my area of expertize." Getting up again from the settee Raena continued, "I really do wish you luck though." Raena still attempting to digest all that Ronnie had just told her, not least the £2m finder's fee, began to hesitate. "And anyway, what makes you think I'd be any help to you?"

Ronnie, still sitting in the enormous armchair, smiled. He half expected it would take a while for Raena to get her head around everything he was telling her. "You underestimate yourself, Raena. You really are quite famous you know. Do you know what the lads at Wormwood Scrubs call you? The Joan of Arc of the underworld. We were all transfixed by the trial. The reports were closely followed by all of us with great interest and, may I say, admiration."

"I'm flattered, Ronnie, but just remember I was found not guilty on both charges."

"We all know that. You did very well. Congratulations."

Raena smiled. She was beginning to take a liking to Ronnie, and the thought of £2m, tax free, was beginning to exercise her imagination. "This £2m, Ronnie, what exactly do you want me to do?"

"Find the diamonds, simple as that. As I've already said you knew Franz Zimmerman, as I did, but I never worked with him, not on a day to day basis like you did. You were there most days, working with him, listening to him with those bugging devices of yours. You must have ideas; his associates for instance. The diamonds haven't just melted away. They're somewhere, not necessarily at Broom Hall, although they could be, but they're somewhere. The arrangement Franz Zimmerman and I made was for me to take the diamonds over to Broom Hall when we got back from Brussels. He was going to show me where they would be hidden. Now I don't know if that was going to be at Broom Hall or somewhere else. Anyway, I gave the diamonds to two of my associates as I had a rather pressing appointment back home which, Debbie, my girlfriend, had texted me about. Unfortunately, the appointment there, with members of Her Majesty's constabulary, resulted in me being offered free accommodation for ten months at Wormwood. Now I'm out I need to find where the diamonds were hidden, simply as that."

Raena was beginning to change her mind. She reckoned she would enjoy working, albeit at a distance, with Ronnie White. At the very least it could be worth considering. "OK, Ronnie, I'm not promising anything, but how about we get together and go over things. I'm away till Sunday so how about you call me then? No earlier than eleven o'clock. I'll be catching up with my beauty sleep. I might need you to update me with some details, then we'll see."

Ronnie got up from the chair and smiled at Raena. "You're some young lady, Raena, my kind of girl. I have a feeling this could be the start of a very profitable association."

"Come on, Ronnie, I'll show you out." Raena handed Ronnie a piece of paper. "Now, before you go just a couple of things. This is my telephone number, so ring me Sunday." Raena held the door open for her very unexpected guest. "Speak to you Sunday, Ronnie."

Ronnie, about to leave turned round. "You said there were a couple of things you wanted to say, Raena?"

"Oh yes. My fees, Ronnie, they'll be £5m."

Ronnie was still smiling as the girl exiting the lift he was about to enter bumped into him. "Oops, sorry," she said as she made her way over to Raena's apartment. "OK, Raena, who was that tall, rather good-looking guy getting into the lift I bumped into? Another one of your clients I've no doubt, and I thought you'd only just got back from Germany an hour ago. No wonder you've got more money than Barclays Bank."

Raena laughed, after hugging Christine she took her case and put it in the bedroom. She was keen to explain all about the visit she'd just had from Ronnie White, the so-called great diamond robber. Raena was going through all they'd been talking about, her mind still in overdrive.

One of the many frustrating things for Chief Inspector Whiteman when investigating the murder of Franz Zimmerman was the continual interference by officers from Special Branch. They had removed many items from the Hall including, or so Chief Inspector Whiteman believed, several of his diaries in their efforts to prevent the names of some of Zimmerman's more prominent associates reaching the public domain. The entries made in the diaries had all been entered in code. The apparatus used in creating that code, it appeared, had also been taken. However, although Special Branch had removed many items from Broom Hall what they and DCI Whiteman had been unaware of was Raena McCory had taken three of Zimmerman's diaries and the decoding apparatus from the safe in the lounge of Broom Hall when taking the painting. These items, together with the oil painting by Degas, she'd placed in the boot of the car Christine used to drive her friend back to Birmingham Airport to catch her flight to Germany, a flight they'd planned would provide Raena's alibi.

Later that evening, as Raena and Christine were enjoying their second helping of sweet and sour pork and fried rice at the Manderin restaurant, Raena looked across the table at her friend. "OK, Christine, are you game for a bit of excitement?"

"Raena, don't you ever think about anything else but sex?"

Raena laughed. "Not very often, Christine, but this is not about sex, it's about money, a lot of money if you're interested."

"I'm always interested in money, love, you know that, but don't start trying to get me involved in one of your investment schemes. You know me. The only thing I understand about long term investments is the week we spend in Paris every year with that lot from the International Monetary Fund."

"It's nothing to do with business, Chris, but, before I go on, those things I asked you to keep for me, the diaries and that decoding apparatus from Broom Hall, you still have them I hope?"

"Decoding apparatus, is that what it is? Yes, of course I do. You asked me to hang on to them and I have. They're at my flat in Manchester."

"Right, we'll need those to start with, so bring them over to my place on Sunday."

"OK, but are you going to tell me what all this is about?"

Raena, draining the last of her wine from her glass, leaned forward. "That guy you bumped into leaving my place earlier, do you know who he was?"

"I've no idea. One of your tea-time quickies?"

"No, Chris, that was Ronnie White."

Christine shrugged her shoulders. "Never heard of him."

"Well, Ronnie White, Chris, is a very well-known gangster, and he told me it was his lot who carried out that diamond robbery last year at Brussels Airport."

Christine frowned still trying to catch up with what her friend was telling her. Then it suddenly came to her. Putting her chopsticks down on the table she stared at Raena. "The great diamond robbery, the one where all those diamonds were nicked from some aircraft? They're worth millions!"

"Yes, Chris," replied Raena, glancing round the restaurant. "And keep your voice down. Apparently, so he told me, it was Franz Zimmerman who organized the whole thing and, not only that, according to him those diamonds could be hidden somewhere at Broom Hall, either there or close by, but wherever, they are hidden. I've been asked to help find them and, if successful, there's a few million pounds of reward money waiting. Now, I remember on one of my bugging devices a telephone conversation Zimmerman was having with someone. He was discussing details of a consignment of diamonds which would need cutting and then putting up for sale. I threw all the discs in the waste bin when I got back home from court but, luckily, the next morning I changed my mind. I got them out of the bin and put them away. So tonight we make a start by going through the recordings. Then, on Sunday, we get together with those diaries and the decoding apparatus and see what we can find. There's a lot of money to be earned here, Chris, if we're successful, and you know me, I always like to be successful."

Chapter 11

Sheila, taking another swig of coffee, picked up her keys and was about to leave for the station when her mobile rang. It was Greg. "Some cheeky bastard's nicked my car! Can you give me lift?"

"Yes, if you're ready now. I'm just about to leave."

"Yes, OK then. I'll get something at the canteen later."

"Have you reported it, Greg?" said Sheila as they drove along the Stratford Road towards the city.

"Not yet, I'll do it when we get to Birmingham. Obviously some joyriders, Sheila. No one would pinch my car for any other reason, would they?"

"I hope you hadn't left any papers in there. You know what you're like."

Greg, about to light a cigarette, removed the weed from his lips. "The only papers in there were a week's collection of McDonald's cartons and about a dozen empty cigarette packets."

"Well I hope you're right and, by the way no smoking if you don't mind."

"No coffee, no fags, I'll be a nervous wreck before lunchtime."

"It'll do you good, and don't forget we've a busy morning ahead of us. DI Partridge and that Inspector from Brussels are due at the office first thing, so make sure everyone's ready for the meeting. I'll need to speak with our beloved superintendent before we kick off, so no time for messing about."

Greg, looking out of the passenger window, was beginning to regret calling Sheila for a lift. He was thinking to himself that he could have turned up at the station a couple of hours later with the perfect excuse that his car had been nicked. I never could think clearly first thing in the morning, he thought. At Birmingham Central Greg went off to get everyone ready for the meeting, followed by a cigarette and coffee while Sheila took the elevator to the superintendent's office.

"Sit down, Sheila, I want to have a word with you before your meeting this morning." Superintendent Davies, moving to one side the pile of papers on his rather modern-looking desk, looked over at Sheila. "This Nurse Milligan case, it looks as though there could be a connection not only with that diamond robbery at Brussels last year but with Franz Zimmerman as well. I've had a call from the Chief Constable this morning who's asked to be kept up to date on things, and on a daily basis if necessary, so you'll need to report to me every morning. Now we need to be clear on how we go forward on this one. I'll be at your meeting with DI Partridge and Inspector Claes who, I'm told, should be here around nine o'clock, so make sure everyone's ready to begin." Hesitating for a few moments Superintendent Davies then continued. "You see, Sheila, if there is a connection between the murder of Nurse Milligan and that diamond robbery, and of course Franz Zimmerman, then you know who you'll be coming up against don't you? Special Branch. They are still very much involved in going over Zimmerman's past, so you need to be aware of that."

Returning to her office Sheila still thought her superintendent looked out of place in his new office with all the retro style furniture and accessories. Being one of the old-fashioned, traditional-looking coppers, she smiled to herself. He looked so much more at home with the old oak, chunky style furniture we had at the Digbeth office, not all that black and silver- coloured retro gear, she thought.

"OK, Greg, no doubt you've had a fag by now so go and tell everyone the meeting is to start soon. DI Partridge and Inspector Claes are due to arrive shortly and the Super will be joining us so watch your language this morning. Apparently the Milligan enquiry has caught the interest of the Chief Constable as well."

Greg looked at his watch. "I've got time for another coffee and a fag, Sheila, see you in a bit."

"Have you reported your car being stolen yet?"

Stopping at the door to Sheila's office Greg turned round with a broad grin on his face. "It's been found burnt out in Acocks Green.

I can get a new one now when the insurance money comes through."

"OK, well hurry up with your cigarette. I'll want to go over a couple of things with you before DI Partridge and Inspector Claes arrives."

The meeting started promptly in the incident room at nine thirty. DI Partridge had introduced Inspector Claes to Sheila and her team after arriving at Birmingham half an hour previously. This had given everyone the opportunity of updating each other with their respective enquiries.

Sheila began the meeting. "You've all had the opportunity of welcoming Inspector Claes from the Brussels Federal Police, and of course DI Partridge from the Met who most of you know already. Now it's looking more and more likely that the shooting of Nurse Milligan could be somehow connected to a diamond robbery which took place at Brussels Airport last year. Inspector Claes is in charge of that investigation. Now there's nothing definite yet, but I believe there's enough for both of us to work on that possibility for a while."

Turning to Inspector Claes, Sheila nodded for him to update everyone with his investigation. Inspector Claes, thought Sheila, was not a Hercule Poirot, quite the opposite in fact, more like a young version of Columbo. Inspector Claes stood up to address the meeting. Wearing an extremely ill-fitting suit, and a shirt which looked as though it had yet to make its acquaintance with the ironing board, Inspector Claes ran his fingers through his mop of disheveled-looking hair as he prepared to address the meeting. His very charming and extremely knowledgeable and detailed report of his investigation into the Brussels diamond robbery quickly dispelled any doubts anyone may have had about his ability or qualifications. His detailed and professional summary of his investigation quickly overshadowed the somewhat obvious distractions made by his appearance. In perfect English Inspector Claes continued his report.

"My colleagues and I at Brussels have no doubt now the robbery was an inside job. We believe the anonymous tip-off received a few days after the robbery naming Zimmerman as the organizer came from one of Zimmerman's associates, an Antoine Lemarchal, who, we understand, fell out with Franz Zimmerman in a big way a few years back over some business deal which went very expensively wrong for him. Now Lemarchal resides in Paris. However, so far we've been unable to trace him. We've also been unable to track down two members of the gang who we now know were involved in the robbery. Fingerprints of William Spears and George McCann were found on cartons taken from the aircraft, but both Spears and McCann have also disappeared. We also believe the gang leader, one of Zimmerman's long-standing associates, a Ronnie White, who, incidentally has recently moved to an address in one of your Cotswold villages not far from Zimmerman's old residence at Broom Hall. A village called Moreton-in-Marsh. Now we've purposely delayed making contact with the aforementioned Mr. White until we have a little more to go on. We don't want him doing a disappearing act as well. As you may be aware Ronnie White has for the last ten months or so been held at your prison, Wormwood Scrubs, but was released a few days ago so perhaps surveillance of Mr. White can now be arranged. We're not surprised the diamonds have yet to make an appearance, we assumed they'd be hidden away for quite a while. However, there are three things which puzzles me. Firstly, the disappearance of both William Spears and George McCann immediately after the robbery, secondly, the tip-off we received naming Franz Zimmerman as the brains behind the scheme, and thirdly, the complete lack of any information from any of our usual sources. With an incident as big as the robbery at Brussels there's always someone ready to offer information, valid or otherwise, but with this there's been an unusual silence, absolutely nothing at all. DI Partridge has updated me with the events at Broom Hall last year and informed me of some of Zimmerman's activities, and his association with the organization, the Knights Templar. However, my interest here is in solving the theft of the diamonds and gold taken from the Helvetic Airways plane at Brussels Airport on the 14th of June last year, nothing more."

Sheila thanked Inspector Claes for his update. "Right, everyone, we need to work with Inspector Claes which may also help us in our investigation into the shooting of Nurse Milligan. As I've already mentioned it looks likely the two incidents could be connected. I agree with Inspector Claes about arranging surveillance on Ronnie White. We need a twenty-four hour surveillance on him to be arranged immediately. If he, as Inspector Claes suspects, was involved in the theft of the diamonds, then sooner or later we can assume he'll make contact with the other members of his gang. When he does, hopefully, that will lead us not only to the diamonds but possibly the murderer of Nurse Milligan as well. So, DI Goode, I want you to arrange the surveillance of Ronnie White, round the clock for the moment, and get clearance for tapping his phones. Sergeant Ryan, I want you to go through the passenger lists of everyone flying to and from Brussels two weeks before and two weeks after the robbery. As we are all aware Ronnie was on parole at the time of the robbery so he'd have had to have used a false passport. Go through the lists of all the passengers and check them out. It's very likely the other members of his gang were also traveling with false identities. Constable Finmore, I want you to organize this. Now, Sergeant Ryan and Inspector Goode, you both saw the interview with Andrew Williams. What were your impressions?"

Inspector Goode, picking up some notes from the table, looked over to Sheila. "I felt he was hiding something. His explanations on things for me didn't quite ring true. For instance, why didn't Stephen ask for some of the money he'd lent Andrew to help with his purchase of 14 Carters Close. Wasn't it £5,000 he told us? OK, we all know Stephen was supposed to be hopeless with his finances but surely even he would have understood he was three months in arrears with his rent and, not only that, he'd got the bank on his back demanding his overdraft be reduced. It just doesn't ring true that Stephen hadn't asked Andrew for at least some help to sort things out. He and Stephen were supposed to be very close so why didn't he ask him, or if Andrew was aware of Stephen's predicament why didn't he offer? We know Andrew was reasonably OK for money. Even after purchasing the property at Carters Close he could still have afforded a couple of grand to help out his friend. Then the disappearance of Billy Spears from the hospital, I find it hard to believe he didn't know more about that and the £25,000. He just seemed to me to be portraying the innocent bystander, and I have a problem with that."

"OK, Sergent, what are your opinions?"

"About the same as Inspector Goode. I think it's very likely Andrew knows more than he's letting on. When I checked again on Stephen's account with the Coventry Building Society, there was no £5,000 withdrawn from Stephen's building society account on or around the time Stephen purchased that property at Carters Close. Monies were regularly withdrawn as we are all aware but nothing of that amount, not around the time he purchased Carters Close anyway. Andrew purchased the property for £160,000 and completion of the transaction took place on the 5th of January this year. I've checked with the conveyancing clerk at Andrew's solicitors. Andrew paid a deposit of £9,000 on the 20th of December 2012. These monies were paid by transfer from his savings account at the Bank of Scotland directly to his solicitors' client account."

"OK, Sergeant, I think we need another chat with Andrew Williams which Greg and I will do this afternoon." Sheila, picking up the pile of papers on the table looked round the room. "Any other comments?" Then turning to Superintendent Davies, "We can accommodate DI Partridge and Inspector Claes here for a while if that's OK, sir. I think together we just might be able to assist each other in both these enquiries. Meanwhile Greg and I will have another chat with Andrew Williams. Right, if there are no further questions let's get on with things. We'll meet back here at five o'clock this evening."

As Sheila began to make her way back to her office, Superintendent Davies beckoned to her. "A quick word, Sheila, before you go off. In my office, ten minutes."

Superintendent Davies thought Sheila, looked somewhat concerned as he began his so-called 'quick word'. Getting up from his desk he wandered over to the large picture windows overlooking Birmingham City. "I'm glad to see you're beginning to settle in here, Sheila, and getting on with everyone, not least of all DI Goode who I know from experience can be a bit of a handful at times." Turning away from the window Superintendent Davies looked down at the floor as he walked slowly back to his desk. "These two cases, the diamond robbery and the shooting of Nurse Milligan, one or both of them may have the interest of Special Branch. Now, I'm not sure for certain, but a few things the Chief Constable told me this morning, or perhaps more precisely a few things he didn't say, makes me think there may well be something going on behind the scenes."

Sheila smiled, "One day I might just have a simple case of murder or robbery to investigate without Special Branch or anyone else tiptoeing around me. Are they interested because of the possible connection with Zimmerman, or is there something else I should be aware of?"

"I'm not sure, Sheila. It just may be because Zimmerman was the architect of the diamond robbery and, as we're all aware, Whitehall is still very much involved with the Zimmerman investigation. You just need to be aware Special Branch just may be involved, so watch your back."

After what, rather surprisingly, thought Sheila, did turn out to be just a 'quick word' with her superintendent, she took the elevator back down to the second floor to the main office. Making her way over to her office, Greg rather hurriedly came over to her.

"We can forget about any interview with Andrew Williams, Sheila. He was found dead, half an hour ago, at his house in Carters Close. Shot through the back of the head apparently."

Sheila went into her office and sat down at the desk. Ignoring all the files and paperwork needing her attention she leant back in her chair deep in thought. What the hell was all this about? She'd sensed straight away the shooting of Stephen Milligan was going to be anything but straightforward. A hard-working nurse liked by all his colleagues shot by what looked like the work of a professional hitman. Now his colleague and friend, Andrew Williams, shot by what appeared from first reports to be in exactly the same manner. There was also the disappearance of Billy Spears from the A & E ward at the Queen Elizabeth Hospital, and the disappearance of his associate, George McCann, both of them apparently suffering from some sort of viral infection. Now all this was attracting the attention of Special Branch. It was only just over a year ago Franz Zimmerman, son of a former SS officer, was found dead with a sword through him in the lounge of his residence at Broom Hall. The fallout from all that was still keeping Special Branch busy, and probably other interested parties higher up the chain. But the disappearance of two members of the gang involved in the diamond robbery at Brussels Airport last year, and the shooting of two nurses by what appeared to be the work of a professional hitman? What the hell was going on here?

Chapter 12

The sound of the alarm on the bedside cabinet woke Raena at eight thirty. Throwing back the quilt she slid her naked body from the mattress and walked down the hallway to the bathroom. After her usual morning shower she slipped on a pair of jeans and a T-shirt and went into the kitchen. A strong black cup of coffee, she thought, and I'll have one of those donuts I brought back from New York. Sitting at the breakfast bar Raena began to go over things and plan the day ahead. Having completed her report last night for her client in Manchester, she felt comfortable in recommending they make an offer to purchase the business. After meeting the administrators in New York on Thursday, it was up to her client now whether to proceed with an offer or not. Raena felt confident the business could be a good investment. Whoever took over would need to make some redundancies and close around a dozen of the eighty shops in the chain. She also recommended they specialize a little more; take in more profitable lines. Eighteen months down the line it could be a very viable proposition. Staring out of the window overlooking the grounds of Worcester Apartments she completed her first meal of the day, then, grabbing her cigarettes and lighter, walked back down the hallway into the lounge. The phone rang. It was Ronnie White. "Can't hear you very well, Ronnie," said Raena, as she attempted to push the phone even closer to her ear.

"I'm in a call box, love. Being watched by the local constabulary at the moment so it's best we don't make contact for a while. I'll contact you soon, Raena."

"Don't worry, Ronnie, I'm starting on our project today. Give me a shout in a few days time."

It was Sunday and Raena was keen to commence the search for the diamonds Ronnie White and his gang had lifted from the aircraft at Brussels Airport the previous year. A bit of a wild card, she thought to herself, but you never know, there could be a lot of money to earn here. Besides, Raena could never resist the temptation of a challenge, especially one offering a reward of several million. She was a brilliant business consultant and investor. Her natural aptitude in seeing opportunities in the world of finance were helped in no small way by her part-time occupation as a high-class hooker. This second part-time occupation not only provided a very substantial income while waiting for her investments to materialize, but also brought her into contact with leading bankers, politicians, business moguls and celebrities from all walks of life. Her assortment of bugging devices, as she saw them, were the icing on the cake. They provided her with the invaluable inside information she needed. It was these devices she'd used at Broom Hall which, she hoped, may give her information as to where Zimmerman had planned to hide the diamonds. In business, as in her personal life, Raena's success was in no small way due to the way she thought through and planned her every move. Her natural aptitude for creative thinking and attention to every detail had over the years brought many rewards. During the time at Broom Hall, Raena recalled the meetings Zimmerman had with many of his associates. It was possible, she thought, her bugging devices may just have caught something. However, there would be many hours of recordings held on the devices. She needed to shortcut the process of listening to all those. Placing the discs into her word finder she typed in five key words for the computer to locate. *Diamonds – Brussels – Airport – Ronnie - White.* She placed the discs into the machine. Leaving the apparatus to do its work Raena turned on her laptop, went into Google and typed in *Diamond Robbery, Brussels Airport.* There must be, thought Raena, over fifty listings at least, all detailing what was regarded as the biggest and most audacious robbery ever. Reading the reports, Raena learnt it took just minutes for six armed men dressed as police officers to pull up alongside Helvetica Airways flight number LX799, break into the cargo hatch and take off with cartons containing an estimated £90m of uncut diamonds, and around another £10m of gold bullion. The robbers, using two black Mercedes vans and a black Audi saloon all fitted with blue flashing lights, drove off the runway and through the gap they'd made a few minutes earlier in the perimeter fencing. The vehicles were found later, burnt out, some three miles from the airport. Because of the heist's clockwork precision there was speculation the job was an inside operation, and may even have been the work of a terrorist organization. The Brussels Federal Police, however, confirmed only that the investigation was ongoing. The reports all seemed to agree that the thieves were obviously aware it would have been far too risky to have made their move in Antwerp.

Antwerp, being the world's capital for diamond cutting, situated just forty-three kilometers (twenty-seven miles) from Brussels Airport, had security second to none. The city's diamond industry had some two thousand surveillance cameras, police monitoring and countless identity controls to protect its daily £200m trade of rough and cut diamonds. The world's diamond center spokeswoman Caroline De Wolf said, "Antwerp's security operation is without doubt the safest and most comprehensive in the world."

"Which is why Ronnie and company decided on Brussels Airport," said Raena to herself as she lit another cigarette. After checking the word finder apparatus she found that all five words had been found at various times on the recordings she'd made at Broom Hall. Could be getting somewhere, she thought as the intercom buzzed. It was Christine Henderson.

"Are you going to give me a hand with these books and this bloody typewriter contraption?" Raena saw her friend on the video screen looking decidedly fed up waiting at the main entrance with two large boxes at her side.

"OK, Chris, don't panic, I'm on my way down." After helping Christine with the decoding apparatus and the case containing the diaries, she made two coffees and sat back in the lounge with her friend. Raena began to update Christine with her progress so far. "Definitely an inside job, Chris, no doubt in my mind about that. Now according to Ronnie, when they got back to England being unaware Franz Zimmerman was dead, he told George McCann and Billy Spears to take the diamonds straight over to Broom Hall while he carried on back home to meet with the local police who were waiting for him about some unrelated matter. Now what Ronnie and his associates were unaware of at the time was Zimmerman was dead. So, when George and Billy arrived at Broom Hall who did they meet there? And more importantly where did they hide the haul of diamonds? Ronnie's convinced there was no way they'd have attempted doing a runner so, that being the case, where the hell would they hide £90m worth of uncut diamonds, and who met them and showed them where to hide them?"

"Wouldn't they have gone over to Ronnie's place, or called him?"

"No, Chris, Ronnie had told them the police were waiting for him. That would have been the last place they'd go."

"Well, as I see it, Raena, all this gear I've humped down here from Manchester is not going to be any help is it? As soon as George and this Billy character became aware of the goings on at Broom Hall then, if they didn't do a runner, they'd have certainly hidden the diamonds somewhere far away from Broom Hall and, my guess is, waited for things to cool down before going back to get them. So, to be honest, how the hell are you, or anyone else for that matter, going to find out where they are now? The only way is for your Ronnie White to find these characters and ask them. And that job is not exactly in your line of business, and it's certainly not in mine. I can't help thinking, love, despite the very attractive finder's fee you say has been offered, this is going to turn out to be a complete waste of time."

Raena was thinking hard. Staring out of the window overlooking Worcester Cathedral she turned to her friend. "I hear what you say, Chris, but Ronnie White contacts me to help find the diamonds, right? Now, he's an intelligent guy, he's no fool, and he's had some ten months or so to think things through. I reckon he believes the clue to where the diamonds could be hidden is in the recordings or the diaries he assumes I've still got. Well he's right about that. We do have the recordings and the diaries, so we listen to the recordings and go through the diaries and then maybe have another chat with him. Let's not give up just yet." Raena, lighting her third cigarette of the morning, sat back down on the settee. "First, let's listen to the recordings which contain the words I put into the computer earlier. There are three conversations noted that Franz Zimmerman had with Ronnie White which contains these words. The first was May 2011, the second, a year later, May 2012 and the third, the 7th of June 2012, just a week before the robbery took place. The recordings were made when Ronnie White had presumably called at Broom Hall to go over some last minute details. So let's make a start and see what we can get from all this. We've got three enormous diaries, Zimmerman's decoding apparatus and my bugging devices. The answer has got to be here somewhere."

Chapter 13

At Birmingham Central Sheila had been busy attempting to catch up with all the paperwork built up over the previous week. The murders of Nurse Milligan and his friend Andrew Williams and, not least of all, the move to Birmingham Central had taken precedence over pretty well everything else. "Bloody pen-pushing!" as Sheila often called it. However, she was aware this was the one part of the job all officers just had to deal with, especially those who'd achieved the rank of chief inspector.

Sheila's partner, John Scarsbrook QC, had returned home for the weekend from his work at the Old Bailey defending an illegal immigrant from Poland who'd been charged with two counts of murder. Two members of his family had been found with their throats cut, and the Crown Prosecution Service, with what appeared to be a very strong case, brought the charges against Ayden Pawlowski last May. John was convinced of his client's innocence but was aware he was not only working against a mountain of evidence but a definite bias towards his client from more than one quarter. This was just the sort of situation which seemed to bring out the best in him. He'd use all his expertize to win the day and prove his client's innocence, but he was aware the outcome was far from certain.

On Sunday John persuaded Sheila to take a break for the day and enjoy some time for themselves. After a late breakfast at their favorite restaurant, the Lygon Arms in the idyllic Cotswold village of Broadway, he and Sheila drove over to Leamington Spa. An early birthday present for Sheila is what he had in mind. He loved Sheila and missed her when working away from home, a situation he was determined to change. He was planning to rearrange his work schedule and concentrate more on corporate business and less on criminal law. The government's planned reduction in the legal aid bill was, in any case, going to change the way his company operated. John was a brilliant advocate and highly regarded within his profession. He'd even been described on more than one occasion as 'The Magician', quite capable of making concrete evidence disappear in front of a jury's eyes, like snow on a summer's day. His good looks – he was often described as a Harrison Ford double – together with his highly accomplished repertoire in the courtroom made him a highly regarded and successful advocate. John had worked on a few occasions for the security services, managing on one occasion to secure a not guilty verdict for an MI5 agent facing a charge of murder. The head of MI5 decided to use John's expertize to clear the matter in a court of law rather than any of the other alternatives at his disposal. John had been approached on a couple of occasions to consider working with the Secret Intelligence Service, once as a young graduate at Cambridge and again a few years later when setting up his offices in Birmingham. He quickly saw through the *façade* of glamour and excitement which had attracted some of his colleagues. A life of intrigue and excitement was not for him. There existed, however, a mutual respect between him and his contacts at MI5 and Special Branch, he was more than happy to help from time to time, albeit in a low-key manner.

Arriving in Leamington Spa John parked his Bentley, which, he reminded himself, was another thing he'd missed. The London Underground and taxi services were not his favorite modes of transport.

Having parked his pride and joy he took Sheila's hand. "Come on, I've a surprise for you." Sheila, trying to keep up with John's fast paced walking, wondered what on earth this was all about. Five minutes later, walking down the Royal Arcade, John stopped outside Salloways, the jewelers. Holding Sheila's hand he pulled her closer to him, then pointing in the window he turned to her. "What do you think of the bracelet on the top of the stand, there in the center of the window?" Sheila looked at the glittering display of jewelry all so perfectly arranged. On the top of the stand, taking center place in the window, Sheila's eyes fell upon the most stunningly beautiful diamond and emerald bracelet.

"Same stones as my engagement ring. It must cost a fortune. You're not seriously offering to buy me that are you?" Sheila with eyes wide open stared at John. "Are you?" she eagerly asked again.

John smiled, "Well not without the matching necklace on the stand next to it. You couldn't really have one without the other could you?"

Walking into the immaculate air-conditioned premises, John and Sheila were met by Charles Salloway, the owner. "Good to see you again, Mr. Scarsbrook. How can we help you this afternoon?"

"The bracelet and necklace you showed me the last time I called. May my wife take a closer look?"

"Most certainly, and this must be the lovely Mrs. Scarsbrook," said Charles with a broad smile. Sheila, still somewhat lost for words, nodded and returned the smile. After carefully taking the two items from the window, Charles laid them on a black velvet cloth on top of the main counter. Standing back he invited Sheila to examine them. "Please, Mrs. Scarsbrook, try them on. There is a mirror over there."

Sheila, feeling as though she'd just been given the keys to Aladdin's cave took off her watch, then draped the heavy white gold diamond and emerald studded bracelet over her wrist and closed the security catch. The necklace was next. Staring at herself in the mirror she could hardly believe her eyes. The excitement, she thought, was almost unreal. Turning to John, "Is this really my birthday present?"

"Yes, and no arguments." For a few brief moments all the tensions of the past couple of weeks seemed to disappear. The move to Birmingham Central, the murders of Stephen Milligan and Andrew Williams, all the pressures of being a detective chief inspector in the country's second city seemed a long way away. Sheila felt excited, happy and so lucky to have met and fallen in love with the man standing next to her. After settling the account John turned to Sheila. "Come on, let's go and get something to eat."

Sheila wasn't hungry. After all the excitement and the enormous breakfast at the Lygon Arms a few hours earlier she doubted she could eat anything until at least suppertime. "John, I'm full, absolutely full. I couldn't eat another thing."

"OK, well let's go and get a coffee somewhere and you can update me on how things are progressing at your new offices."

The Hampton Tea Rooms, a small and perfectly run restaurant situated just outside Leamington Spa, made the ideal stop-off. Starched white tablecloths, all perfectly ironed, covered the dozen or so tables each with a silver vase holding a set of four perfectly arranged roses.

Not too many customers, and great coffee and biscuits, thought John. "OK, Sheila, how did the first week at Birmingham Central go? Greg behaving himself I hope."

Sheila smiled. "He's OK. I don't think anything would upset him. His car was stolen the other day; seemed pleased as punch when it was found a few miles away burnt out. He's eagerly waiting for the insurance to pay up so he can go and get himself something else."

John smiled. "I thought you were all supplied with vehicles."

"We are but Greg always being different takes the allowance instead."

"And how are the new offices? Everyone settling in OK?"

"Actually a lot better than I thought, although none of us have had much time to familiarize ourselves with the place yet. Two nurses found shot dead have kept us all pretty busy."

John looked somewhat surprised. "Two nurses murdered? That sounds a little different from the norm."

"Yes, it looks as though there could be a connection to a diamond robbery carried out at Brussels Airport last year. We have an Inspector Claes from the Brussels Federal Police over here, and our old friend Inspector Partridge from the Met working with us at the moment."

"I remember the diamond robbery, Sheila, one of the biggest robberies ever, apparently." John pouring himself another coffee from the very elegant glass percolator looked in deep thought. "There was speculation the robbery was possibly organized by some terrorist organization."

"I'm not sure about that, John. According to Inspector Claes they had a tip-off that it had been organized by our old friend Franz Zimmerman."

"So what's the connection then with the shooting of the nurses?" Sheila explained the incident with Billy Spears who collapsed at the Queen Elizabeth Hospital and the £25,000 Stephen Milligan had come into shortly afterwards. "So you reckon a member of the gang could have silenced the nurses because they knew too much?"

"Something like that may have happened. All I know is Superintendent Davies has hinted I've probably got Special Branch tiptoeing around me, and not to mention Inspector Claes and Inspector Partridge. Anyway, where did you hear there could be a terrorist connection?"

"One of my pals at Special Branch mentioned it. When the robbery took place, as no doubt you'll remember, it was big news everywhere. We were having a drink one evening and he reckoned it could have been some terrorist organization who'd organized the whole thing. I shouldn't take too much notice. It was only speculation. Pub talk you know."

"Well, I'd be really grateful if you can have another chat with your friend, see if you can't pick his brains a little."

John smiled. "I'll ask, but don't hold your breath. Meanwhile, what's your next move, Sheila?"

"Make contact with all the associates and relatives of Billy Spears and George McCann. Someone's got to know something, or at least have an idea what the connection is with the murders of those nurses."

John looked at Sheila. She really was so very beautiful. Her long blonde hair seemed to caress her shoulders. Her deep blue eyes, the way she carried her tall, slim elegant figure. John smiled to himself. She really couldn't look anything less like a chief inspector of Her Majesty's constabulary. More like a supermodel from *Vogue* magazine. But she needed to relax a little more. Finishing his coffee John placed the cup back in the saucer. "Right, next Wednesday is your birthday. Now, as you know I can't get back from London on Wednesday. I'll be making my closing speech to the jury on Thursday so we'll all be working flat out on all that, but Friday, after the judges summing up, we'll celebrate with a meal out somewhere. We could pop over to Paris for the weekend. What do you think?"

Sheila took John's hand and smiled. "I'm in the middle of a double murder enquiry."

"And I'm in the middle of a murder trial, but we make time for ourselves, Sheila. I'll book us a room at the Hotel Bel Ami. You remember we stayed there last year for a couple days. We always said we'd go back one day?"

Sheila smiled and looked at John. She was about to say she couldn't take the time away from her work, but after thinking for a moment, said, "Your right. Let's have a couple of days to ourselves. Let's go mad, and thank you so much for the lovely bracelet and necklace. They are just so lovely. What would I do without you?"

"Probably work eighteen hours or more a day instead of the twelve or so you do already."

Chapter 14

Raena walked into her lounge holding two cups of freshly made coffee. Handing one to Christine she lit a cigarette then stretched herself out on the settee. Her very expensive designer coffee table was buried beneath a pile of papers, two laptops, two large glass ashtrays and several box files. Raena and her friend Christine had both been working pretty well non-stop all day. The bugging devices, the entries in Zimmerman's diaries, which they'd carefully translated using the decoding apparatus, had all begun to reveal the plans Zimmerman had been making to organize one of the biggest robberies of all time. Surprisingly though, thought Raena, there seems very little detail. The entries in Zimmerman's diaries simply referred to Ronnie White's visits to Broom Hall to run over the basic outline of the planned heist, but very little else.

Raena recalled how Zimmerman very rarely discussed any of his business activities, and never wrote anything down. He used to boast how his head was his office, his computer and his calculator, in fact his whole organization. "All in here," he would say tapping his forehead. "No one has access but me."

So, thought Raena, even the coded entries he made in his diaries were brief and kept to a minimum. However, a pattern of sorts was beginning to emerge. The first reference to any transport of diamonds being made from Antwerp to Zurich was entered in Zimmerman's diary some three years before the robbery took place, September 2009. A company called Domino Mining Ltd made a delivery, according to Zimmerman's notes, every two months or so. The name Domino Mining seemed to ring a distant memory for Raena, but she couldn't quite remember why. If it's important I'll probably remember, she thought. The bugging devices simply suggested Zimmerman was the brains behind the robbery. However, the recorded conversations with Ronnie White were almost as brief as the diary notes.

Christine, busy working at the decoding apparatus, had got to the last entry made in Zimmerman's diary, the night he was murdered on the 14th of June 2012. She carefully entered the text of the entry into the decoding machine and then looked at the message. "Could have something here, Raena, love. Entry made on the 14th of June last year. It reads, *Success, diamonds arrive tomorrow. Bernard to organize delivery to Bush Fm. 10am.*"

Raena took the paper from Christine and looked at the typewritten note. "Bernard, that's Zimmerman's son, the younger one. And Bush Fm, that's got to be short for Bush Farm." Sitting back at her laptop Raena typed into Google, *Bush Farm, North Cotswolds.* "Let's see if there's a Bush Farm round here." Several appeared, three in Northumberland, two situated just outside Norwich but one literally a few miles from Broom Hall. *Bush Farm Holidays, log cabins, stone cottages, all self-catering, available for parties of 2–40 guests. Also Christmas holidays a speciality.* Raena felt excited. "Chris, you're right, love, this could be what we've been looking for. We just might have something here. Bush Farm, unless I'm very much mistaken, was one of Zimmerman's companies, or at least one he had an interest in. It's a big place," said Raena, staring at the screen of her laptop. "Twenty acres or so. Bush Farm, Moreton-in-Marsh." Now the name of that mining company in Antwerp, thought Raena, that name also rings a bell. She typed into Google, *Domino Mining Ltd.* There were several entries but one immediately caught Raena's eye.

Domino Mining Ltd, which operates the Evenlode Mine, reported that revenue from the sale of rough diamonds reached $25 million in the second quarter of the current trading year. Operating expenses totaled $14 million leaving a profit of $11 million. The company was now beginning to show a remarkable turnaround from the previous three years trading accounts which had shown a total loss of $57 million. An average loss per year of $19 million.

According to Alan Alexander, the executive chairman, the recovery had been due to Domino Mining completing its purchase of Kingstone Mining in February this year, twelve months earlier than had been expected. This had been achieved by the early debt repayments totaling $42m. The company stated that eighty per cent of the increase in turnover was due to the take off agreement Kingstone Mining had with Tiffany & Co for the mine's fancy yellow diamonds.

"I knew I'd heard the name before. I now remember Zimmerman mentioning it to me once. It could even be one of the companies he'd invested in years ago. The crafty old sod looks like he'd arranged to nick his own diamonds."

Christine looked puzzled. "What! You mean to say he nicked his own diamonds? What for? What good would that do him?"

"He gets the insurance money, Chris, and keeps the diamonds. Doubles his money in one go. Now all we've got to do is find out where they're hidden. I'd like to have a chat with Bernard but I doubt I'd get very far with him." Raena thought for a while. She looked again at the trading figures for Domino Mining detailed on Google. She felt something didn't add up.

Christine saw the strained expression on her friend's face. "What is it, Raena? You look puzzled, love."

Looking up from the computer screen Raena stared out of the lounge window. Then talking aloud to herself, "If Domino Mining Ltd purchased Kingstone Mining in February this year for over a £100m then something doesn't make sense. It says here the insurance payout to Domino Mining Ltd was finally agreed in May this year after what had been a long and drawn out battle with their insurers. Not only that, but from the brief description here on their last three years trading accounts, I can't for the life of me see how they raised £100m in February. Even after receiving the £90m insurance payout, from first glance at the figures quoted they'd still be at least £50m short."

Christine slumped herself on the settee, her long slim legs slipping out of her tunic. Rubbing her eyes she pushed her head back into the cushions and looked at Raena. "Wherever they got the money from that's nothing to do with us, is it?"

"No, your right, Chris," said Raena closing her laptop. "It's just that I like things to stack up so to speak, especially where company finances are concerned." She looked at her friend. "But your right, love, let's concentrate on finding those bloody diamonds. It may not be that complicated. If Zimmerman planned to stash the diamonds somewhere at Bush Farm then perhaps we ought to have a look around the place. How do you fancy a couple of days holiday, Chris?"

"Well, if you're paying, love, count me in."

Raena looked again at the notes she'd been making. "You see, the other thing is, if Ronnie's guys called at Broom Hall at around ten o'clock on the morning of the 15th of June they'd have had no idea Zimmerman was dead. His body wasn't found until the afternoon; the police weren't called until later that afternoon. So, if what's his name, William Spears, and his sidekick arrived at Broom Hall at around ten o'clock, then who told them Bush Farm was where Zimmerman wanted the diamonds hidden? Bernard Zimmerman, or someone, must have taken them there. I think we need to have another chat with Ronnie. We need to know what time he returned home. He only lives a few miles away from Broom Hall so it should have been about the same time his guys arrived there. However, it's a bit difficult to get in touch with him. According to his telephone conversation this morning he's being watched at the moment, so we'll go and spend a couple of days at Bush Farm, see what we might find." Raena looked over at Christine. "And don't forget, not a word about Bush Farm, or anything else, to anyone."

Chapter 15

Monday mornings always seemed to follow the same pattern for Sheila. An early start to see how much of the paperwork she could manage to clear before her team arrived. The Sunday break with John had done her the world of good. She felt rejuvenated, and excited about the weekend in Paris they'd planned. Two days in Paris, she kept thinking to herself. She'd wear the birthday present John had bought her, the diamond and emerald bracelet and necklace. I might even get a new dress, she thought, but now I need to get this bloody desk cleared, and then back to the murders of Andrew and Stephen. A bit of old-fashioned legwork is what's required with this case, she thought. It was just turned eight o'clock when Sergeant Ryan and DI Williams arrived. Greg was all smiles. Bet he's got his new car, thought Sheila. "OK, you two," said Sheila, exiting her office, "we have work to do."

"Got my new car, Sheila," said Greg.

I knew it, thought Sheila. "Good, because we have people to interview today so you can do the driving. Sergeant, I need the address of where George McCann was living before he disappeared, and the name of his landlady. Then I want the address of any girlfriend he may have had, and I need the same information for William Spears."

"Got it all together last Friday," handing Sheila the information.

"Thank you, Sergeant. By the way, are Inspector Claes and DI Partridge around?"

"They said they'd be in later. Gone to see one of Franz Zimmerman's associates in Manchester apparently."

"OK, make sure everyone's in the incident room for five o'clock.

We can update with everyone then. Come on, Greg, you can show me your new car."

They took the elevator to the ground floor. Walking over to the allocated parking area Sheila saw what she hoped was not Greg's new mode of transport. The nearer they got, however, the more sure she was that the 1970s something Ford Lotus Cortina convertible was Greg's new car. "What do you think, Sheila? An absolute classic. I had one years ago, absolutely loved it. Goes like a rocket."

Oh God, thought Sheila, he's going back in search of his youth. "Well I hope it's reliable. I'm far too busy to have to spend the day talking to the AA."

"The AA? This car you're looking at is one of the most reliable ever made by Ford and Lotus. Over forty years old and can still leave behind most of your new fangled so-called sports cars."

Sheila, removing the two empty cigarette packets from the front seat, climbed in and began to fasten the seatbelt. "I hope these belts are OK. This thing looks as though it was made long before these were thought of."

Greg just smiled. "You're sitting in a piece of motoring history here, part of our heritage. So where to first of all, Sheila? I have the feeling you want to get back to a bit of old-fashioned policing today?"

Yes, thought Sheila, and we're in the right car to do it. "Right, Greg, George McCann's previous address at Summerfield Avenue, Dudley."

"That's the one DI Partridge told us about. What was the landlady's name? Elsie, or something like that?"

"Mrs. Elson, Greg. Jane Elson. And yes, DI Partridge has spoken with her, so let's see what he might have missed, shall we?"

Forty minutes later after what turned out to be a completely uneventful journey, much to Sheila's relief, Greg pulled up outside George McCann's last known address, 14 Summerfield Avenue, a large two-storey Victorian terraced property. They walked up the driveway to the brightly painted orange-coloured front door, to the side of which there were four pushbutton doorbells. Flat 1 (Elson) Flat 2 (Evans) Flat 3 (Peters) Flat 4 (Mathews). Turning round Greg noticed that his beloved car had attracted a couple of young lads who'd been playing football opposite. "I'll be two seconds, Sheila."

Walking back to the car one of the lads looked up at him. "What is it, mister?"

"It is a classic car, a Ford Lotus Cortina," and taking out his warrant card, "and this here says I'm a detective inspector at Birmingham Central, so I wont see any scratches on it when I come back, will I?"

One lad with a cheeky grin looked again at Greg's car, then before running off turned round, "No, it's got enough of those already, mate!"

Sheila smiled to herself. As Greg walked back along the driveway the front door opened. A plump, fifty-something woman stood there scruffily dressed in a long beige-coloured dressing gown. It was obvious she'd just got out of bed. "Can I help you? If you've come about the apartment it's gone."

Sheila held up her warrant card. "Mrs. Elson?"

"Yes, that's me."

"We're from Birmingham Central. I'm Chief Inspector Whiteman and this is Inspector Williams. May we have a word with you?"

With a look of annoyance Mrs. Elson looked at Sheila and then at Greg. "I've spoken to one of your lot already, about a week ago," Hesitating, she continued, "OK, you'd better come in." Mrs. Elson's apartment was on the ground floor at the front of the property.

Previously, thought Sheila, as they walked through from the hallway, this would have been the lounge and dining room. Converted now to a one-bedroom apartment could be OK, she thought, if the place was given a serious clean. That and getting rid of the smell, of what she could only think was some sort of attempt at cooking.

Mrs. Elson clearing some newspapers and magazines from the settee offered Sheila and Greg a seat then, moving a plate from the chair opposite, sat down. "Thank you for seeing us, Mrs. Elson. We understand you had a George McCann staying in one of your apartments last year?"

"Yes, that's right. I've already told all this to the other bloke from your place."

"I appreciate that, Mrs. Elson, but I wanted to ask you a couple of things you might be able to help us with. You told DI Partridge that Mr. McCann was rather poorly and some friends of his took him to hospital. Is that right?"

"Yes, that's right. It was one night last year, June I think. I can't be sure of the exact date without looking it up, but around that time."

"Did you see who it was who took Mr. McCann to hospital?"

"No, it was very early one morning. I wouldn't have known anything about it if it wasn't for the fact I'd just got out of bed to go to the loo. I heard someone by the front door. When I looked out the window I saw Mr. McCann being helped into a car parked opposite. I thought he was drunk, but then I'd remembered he'd been rather poorly. I went out to the hall and the guy who was just about to close the front door behind him said he was sorry if he'd woken me. He said George was not getting any better and he was taking him to hospital."

"Would you recognize the man again, the man you spoke to?"

"No it was dark and, well, it was about three o'clock in the morning so I wasn't exactly taking that much notice. I knew Mr. McCann hadn't been well and thought no more about it."

"Did you see the car he got into?"

"Not really, it was parked over the road. The tenants use the driveway and the space in front of the house to park their cars. It was some sort of estate car. Dark blue colour, I think."

"And the man you say you spoke to, was he young, old, is there anything you can tell me about him?"

"He was a big guy, middle-aged I guess, but apart from that I really couldn't say."

"How long was George a tenant here?"

"Just five months. I remember that because I used his deposit to pay the last months rent when he didn't come back after going to hospital."

"What about his apartment, Mrs. Elson. When he didn't return I assume you checked it out to get it ready for reletting. Was there anything left there, clothes or any personal items?"

"No, there was nothing there at all. He must have come back and took everything away with him when he returned from hospital. The funny thing was it was spotless. He'd thoroughly cleaned the place, or had it cleaned by someone. I remember there was a strong smell of cleaning fluid, bleach of some kind. Never had a tenant go to all that trouble before. You're lucky if they clean anything before they leave."

"And neither you or any of the other tenants saw him again?"

"That's right."

"How long was it before you realized he wasn't returning?"

"About a week, ten days or so, it's not that unusual for tenants to just disappear. I had no way of making contact with him so I let myself into the apartment, and it was then I realized as everything had been cleared he'd obviously moved out."

"What about references, Mrs. Elson, I assume before you let one of your apartments you take references, bank details, employment details, that sort of thing?" Sheila sensed a slight awkwardness in Mrs. Elson. Pulling herself up in the chair she hesitated slightly.

"I found out afterwards they were all false. All the references he gave me didn't exist. My fault I know, but he seemed a nice enough bloke, nicely spoken, smartly dressed, paid three months in advance plus a deposit. I thought he was OK. I didn't bother checking the references he gave me."

"Do you remember what car he drove?"

"He didn't, went everywhere by bus and taxi, or so he said."

"Did anyone call to see him while he was here, girlfriend or business colleagues?"

"Not that I was aware of. I hardly ever saw him to be honest. He only stayed here three or four nights a week, if that."

"The references he gave you, did you keep those?"

"No, I told your other guy who called here that I threw all those away after I realized he'd moved out."

"Did any of your other tenants ever speak to or meet George?"

"Not that I'm aware of. As I've already told you he was hardly ever here. I doubt anyone else even knew the apartment was tenanted."

"I take it all the rents Mr. McCann paid whilst he was here were made in cash?"

Mrs. Elson again looked awkward. "Err...yes."

"And of course, you have to record all these payments and write up the accounts each year for our friends at the Inland Revenue?"

Mrs. Elson was beginning to look even more uncomfortable. "Well, yes, I do."

Sheila smiled. "You must have a good memory remembering all those cash payments being given to you. Are you absolutely sure there's nothing else you can remember about George McCann, anything at all?"

Mrs. Elson rubbing her forehead looked at Sheila. "Well, this is probably nothing at all but the one thing I do remember was when Mr. McCann got back from his holiday, or wherever he'd been last year. I was upstairs checking on the new stair carpet we'd had fitted. I wasn't very pleased with the way it had been laid and was taking a couple of photos on my mobile. I was trying to get a reduction of the bill.

82

Anyway, I was on the landing checking it out at the top of the stairs and I heard George saying he and Billy had done exactly as they'd been told. He was going on about something which had been well and truly buried. Then I heard him say when they want the bloody things back someone else can go down there and get them, not him. Then I heard him say he was feeling bloody awful and was going to bed."

"Was he talking to someone in his room?"

"No, he was on his mobile, he was speaking quite loudly, the reception round here is not that good. I don't know what he was on about but it just sounded a bit dodgy to me. You know, the way he was talking. Anyway, the following evening is when that guy I told you about came over and took him to hospital. And that's everything. There's absolutely nothing else I remember. As I've already told you George McCann was only here three or four nights a week, if that."

"OK, Mrs. Elson. Well, thank you for your help, we might need to speak to you again."

As Sheila got up from the settee Mrs. Elson rather awkwardly looked at her. "I err...suppose the cash payments I've just mentioned, they won't have to be noted will they?"

Sheila smiled. "What cash payments were those, Mrs. Elson?"

"You're a crafty one, Sheila," said Greg pushing the gearstick into first. "Getting Mrs. Elson to open up about the telephone conversation she'd overheard. And what's this about George, or someone, apparently fumigating the apartment before leaving? And the telephone conversation about something being well and truly buried and they could get someone else to collect them when they wanted them back? Were those the diamonds he was talking about?"

"I don't know yet, Greg, but we'll find out eventually."

"Where to now, Sheila?"

"Back to the office. There are a few things I want to check on, then we'll have a word with Sally Peterson."

"Sally Peterson? Who's that?"

"George McCann's old girlfriend. Head of the advertising department at the *Evening Mail* according to what Sergeant Ryan tells me, just round the corner from our offices. So, Greg, you can park your piece of motoring history and we'll walk there. And you can ask the questions this time."

The receptionist at the *Evening Mail* put a call through to Sally

Peterson and asked Sheila and Greg to take a seat. A couple of minutes later Sheila saw who she assumed was Sally Peterson walking across the polished marble flooring of the very impressive reception hall to where she and Greg were sitting. A tall, slim girl, mid-twenties, and if I'm not mistaken, thought Sheila, a right show-off. Greg, however, was taking more notice of the beautiful figure and long legs enhanced by the tight-fitting two-piece suit and high-heeled stilettos which were echoing across the reception area like a burst of firecrackers.

"Sally Peterson? We're from Birmingham Central. I'm DCI Whiteman and this is DI Williams."

Flicking back her hair Sally smiled at Greg. "Detectives, sounds exciting. How can I help you?"

"Is there somewhere we can talk privately for a few moments?"

"Yes, of course, there's an office over here. Follow me." After another burst of firecrackers Sally opened the door to a small interview room next to the main reception area. "We'll be OK in here," she said offering Sheila and Greg a seat. "Nice and private," she said smiling at Greg. Greg was enjoying the view of Sally's long legs which were so obviously being displayed even more by Miss. Peterson as she sat down opposite them.

Greg began his questions. "What can you tell us, Sally, about a boyfriend of yours called George McCann?"

Sally, with a frowned expression, looked at Greg. "He wasn't a boyfriend of mine, just someone I happened to bump into from time to time. We went for a meal once, had a few drinks at the Jeykll and Hyde occasionally, that sort of thing."

"So how would you describe your relationship with him?"

"There wasn't any relationship. He was just someone I spoke with when having a drink after work occasionally. He bought me a drink now and again, we went for a meal once, but that was a bit of a disaster. When we got there George wasn't feeling well so I had to drive him back home. Somewhere in Dudley he lived."

"When was this, Sally?"

"Last year. June if I remember correctly. He'd just got back from holiday and I thought he'd probably caught a bug or something."

"You drove him home, Sally?"

"Yes, he told me he was halfway through a twelve month driving ban for drink driving and didn't want to risk being stopped." Sally looked at

Greg and smiled. "You're probably wondering what the attraction was for me with George. I know he was in his fifties but, if I'm honest, I've always been attracted to the older man, and George McCann, well, he looked interesting, looked as though he had a history. I reckoned there was a lot more behind his rather obvious rugged good looks."

Oh no, thought Sheila to herself, give it a rest. You'll have our Inspector Williams offering you a lift home next in his piece of motoring history.

"Anyway, what's all this about?"

"George McCann seems to have gone missing, Sally, and we're trying to find out what's happened to him."

"Well I haven't seen him since I drove him back home after that meal we were going for. I don't think I can help you very much."

"Well, thank you anyway for your time, Sally. Just one more thing before we leave you in peace. When you drove George home after he said he was feeling poorly, do you remember anything about that? Anything about the symptoms he was complaining of?"

"Not really. The only thing I remember he kept complaining about was a rash or something on his arm. He kept saying it was driving him mad."

"OK, Sally, thank you for your time. We'll get out of your way now."

Walking back to the office Sheila was thinking through a couple of things they'd learnt today when Greg interrupted her thoughts. "Nice girl, Sally, don't you think?"

Sheila, in a rather sarcastic tone was quick to reply. "Oh yes, she was a really lovely girl, Greg."

"I think you're being a little sarcastic, Sheila, but you might be surprised to know there's something else going through my mind at the moment."

"Oh yes and what might that be?"

"Well, firstly, Mrs. Elson's recall of George McCann's telephone conversation. It seemed to suggest he'd buried the diamonds, if that's what he was referring to, and he said, according to Mrs. Elson, when they wanted them back they could get someone else to collect them. Then there is Sally's description of George falling ill on their dinner date. The irritation he was complaining about on his arm. That's what Doctor Khan said he noticed when he examined William Spears the night he disappeared from hospital. He said he'd noticed some burn marks on Spears's right arm. Now both George McCann and William Spears disappeared straight after hiding the diamonds we know they were involved in nicking from that aircraft at Brussels Airport, and the two nurses who we also know examined one of them, William Spears, have been murdered. Not only that but George's landlady described to us how his apartment had been cleaned, virtually fumigated, after he left. When he and William Spears hid the diamonds was there something there they came into contact with, some chemicals or something? And is somebody trying to cover that up? And if so, who? And perhaps more to the point, why?"

"Exactly the same thoughts I was having, Greg. I'm glad Miss. Peterson's rather obvious attempts at flaunting her assets at you didn't completely throw you off course."

"It didn't and we may need to speak with her again."

"I think we have all we need from Miss. Peterson for the moment."

Greg smiled. "You speak for yourself, Sheila."

Chapter 16

Back at the office Sheila began to recap on her thoughts. Were the pattern of events she and Greg could see emerging what actually happened? Was it possible William Spears and George McCann returned with the diamonds from Brussels, had gone and hid them somewhere and, when doing so, came into contact with some sort of chemical which made them ill? The burn marks Doctor Khan noticed on William Spears's arm and Sally Peterson's comment about George complaining about an irritation on his arm before driving him back home when he fell ill on their dinner date seemed to suggest that something like that could have happened. If that was so then why would someone, or some organization, firstly pay £25,000 to keep the nurses who attended William Spears from revealing anything, and then, it would appear, have them murdered when that payment didn't do what they hoped it would? Sheila kept reminding herself all this was nothing more than speculation, but, and this is what worried her, it tied up perfectly with everything they'd learnt so far. The theory did make sense, but it all seemed to point to something which may well be out of her jurisdiction. She again reminded herself it was all, at the moment, just guesswork, nothing else. But she couldn't help going over and over what she and Greg seemed to be uncovering. She was trying to make sense of the rather bizarre series of events surrounding not only the shootings of Stephen and Andrew, but the possible connection there to one of the largest robberies ever to take place. Inspector Claes was investigating the diamond theft. Her investigation was into the murders of the two nurses, Stephen Milligan and Andrew Williams. However, it was beginning to look more and more likely they were looking at two entirely separate incidents which, if her thinking was going along the right lines, were not connected as such. They'd simply overlapped each other. Her instincts also told her she'd need to proceed very carefully. This had all the makings of something which could very easily be taken over by Special Branch before she'd even had the opportunity of getting anywhere near the truth. Sheila kept reminding herself of the three investigations she'd been involved with in recent years that had been snatched away from her because of what had been conveniently called 'National Security'. "Not this time," she said to herself as she sat up in her chair. "Not if I can help it." Even if I have to bend a few rules here, she thought. The first thing is to keep quiet for a while about the theory she and Greg had began to put together before any alarm bells started ringing. I'll need to have a word with him before the meeting at five o'clock, she thought. Seeing Greg exit the elevator she beckoned him to come over. "Close the door, Greg, I need a quick word. I think it's best we keep a few things to ourselves, for the moment anyway. We don't need to mention yet the possibility that George and William became ill because of something they came into contact with when hiding the diamonds. Let's just keep that possibility to ourselves for a while longer."

"I was going to suggest that, Sheila. It would be nice to at least have the chance to find out a bit more before our friends from Special Branch start poking their noses in. We don't know anything for sure but, like you, I have the feeling there's something very sinister behind the murders of those poor sods, Stephen and Andrew."

Sheila couldn't help thinking how her thoughts and instincts very often ran parallel with Greg's. They made a good team. Getting up from her desk she smiled. A very good team, she thought. "OK, Greg, come on. Let's get everyone together and see what else there is to go on."

Inspector Claes is looking a little smarter, thought Sheila. Someone had at least ironed his shirt. Either that or he'd purchased a new one. "How's your investigation going, Inspector?"

"Nothing new at the moment, I'm afraid. I have the feeling this investigation is going to be a long haul. I've been called back to Brussels. The work is building up over there and my boss wants me back so I'm flying out in the morning. As soon as there are any developments here then I'll be back straight away. Meanwhile, I think we're doing things the right way keeping Ronnie White under surveillance. I'm convinced of his involvement in the robbery, but if he gets wind we're on to him he'll simply go to ground. The best chance of learning anything from him is from a distance. What's the saying you have over here, 'give someone lots of rope and they'll hang themselves'?"

Sheila smiled. "Enough rope, Inspector, give someone enough rope and they'll hang themselves."

Inspector Claes smiled. "Ah, yes, I remember now. Your Superintendent Davies is arranging to keep on with the surveillance of Ronnie White so eventually, if we're patient, I have a feeling he may just give us the lead we need."

"Well we've all enjoyed working with you, Inspector, and look forward to working together again very soon. Right, everybody, what else have we got? Inspector Goode did you manage to get anything from Billy Spears's family or friends?"

"Nothing yet, I'm afraid. I managed to speak with a couple of his mates, but nothing. Same with his parents. No one has any idea where he's disappeared to. Either that or they're not saying anything. Everyone's aware of his criminal activities so they're not going to volunteer information to us very easily. However, apart from that I genuinely believe they, like the rest of us, have no idea where he or George McCann have disappeared to. I have one more person I want to speak with, one of his old girlfriends in Manchester. Hopefully I'll be able to track her down tomorrow."

"OK then, Constable Finmore, have you anything?"

"Well, there might be, Sheila. As you know we've been going through all the CCTV footage the night Stephen Milligan was shot. Now, when I interviewed Susan Pearce, the tenant who lives on the ground floor apartment, she told me she'd heard a car starting up at precisely one in the morning the night Andrew was murdered. She remembers the time because it was straight after she'd switched the television off after some film she'd been watching had ended. Now we have footage of a dark blue Audi estate driving along the Bristol Road just two hundred yards from Raddlebarn Court at two minutes past one, just two minutes after Miss. Pearce said she'd heard a car start up at the rear of her apartment. We also have a number of recordings of this vehicle heading south on the M1. Now what we've also discovered, and this is the really exciting bit, is this same vehicle was recorded going through a red light at the junction of the Bristol Road and Oak Tree Lane on the night Billy Spears supposedly signed himself out of the Queen Elizabeth Hospital. And the time this was recorded was just ten minutes after we're told Billy Spears had left the A&E ward."

"You've got the details there have you, Constable?" asked Sheila, attempting not to show her excitement.

"Just waiting for the details now. We only came across all this about half an hour ago."

Sergeant Ryan rather noisily entered the room holding a folder of papers. This could be what we're waiting for, thought Sheila.

"Sorry I'm late, everybody, I just wanted to check on a few things we came across this afternoon and get all this printed out. Has Constable Finmore updated you with the CCTV footage we came across this afternoon?"

"Yes, Sergeant, she has, so what more can you tell us?"

"Quite a bit actually." Sergeant Ryan, obviously excited at what he'd discovered placed the papers on the table, pulled over a chair and sat down. "Right, firstly, we've now discovered that the Audi estate on the CCTV footage is registered to a company based in Bayswater called EBG Pharmaceuticals. The chief executive is a man called Evgeni Berezin, a Russian businessman who moved to this country in 2006 bringing with him his family and most of his £1 billion fortune. I'm only just beginning to get all the details but so far we've learnt that Berezin had apparently fallen out with the Russian authorities in a big way in 2006 over some accusations of tax fraud. Now I don't know whether this bit of information is relevant or not, but according to the information I'm still putting together Evgeni Berezin was, apart from all his business activities, very much associated in an advisory capacity with the KGB. Now he wasn't the driver who jumped the traffic lights. The driver, or at least the one who's on record as committing the offence, was one of Berezin's employees, a Richard Harper. He was fined £60 and had his license endorsed with the usual points. Now what I've also found out is Richard Harper has form. Three convictions for GBH, and one for aggravated burglary. These offences all took place a few years ago. For the last three years we understand he's been employed by Berezin as some sort of minder come chauffeur. He was also known to have worked as a bouncer for a couple of clubs in the West End, but that again was a few years back. Anyway, it now seems he's working for Berezin full time."

"OK, Sergeant, before we all start jumping to conclusions we need to follow up on all this."

Constable Finmore had a question. "Susan Pearce, the tenant on the ground floor at Raddlebarn Court I interviewed the day after Stephen Milligan was murdered. Well she seemed a bit uneasy when I spoke to her. I had the impression she was holding back on something. She was very definite about hearing a car start up the night Stephen was murdered but I just have a feeling she knew more than she was letting on."

"OK, Constable, then you and Sergeant Ryan go over there and have another word with her. And take a photograph of Richard Harper. See if that jogs her memory. Then have another word with all the tenants there. See if any of them ever remember seeing him. Inspector Goode, you're going to track down Billy Spears's ex-girlfriend. I'll be interested to see what you might learn from her. Meanwhile, Greg and I will take a trip down to London and have a word with Richard Harper. We'll meet back here tomorrow at five. OK, that's all for now, and well done everybody, it looks as though there's a chance we could be getting somewhere."

Sheila returned to her office, sat down at her desk and switched on her computer. She wanted as much detail as she could find on the revelations Constable Finmore and Sergeant Ryan had revealed. This was what she loved about her work more than anything else. Going through all the remnants of information left scattered around an investigation it was her task to solve. With her natural, creative thinking, she'd put the pieces together and see what picture emerged. The answers, she kept telling herself, are always there. It was simply a question of rearranging the pieces until they fitted. She was not one for jigsaws or crosswords but her father was addicted to both. He always surrounded himself with newspapers, and when not working on the latest cryptic clues would turn his attention to the boxes of jigsaws containing the hundreds of intricately shaped pieces all needing to be placed in exactly the right position. She remembered as a young child he'd often say the answer to every problem was always there. She remembered him telling her once the answers are created before the clues. Sheila thought that's where her insatiable appetite for solving riddles had originated from. Her Dad would always say lots of mental exercise kept your brain in tune, helped you keep young. Sheila smiled. He was right on that one. He is eighty years old next month, she thought, and very often able to complete *The Sunday Times* cryptic in under five minutes.

After about an hour Sheila picked up the pile of data she'd printed out, placed the couple of dozen pages into her briefcase and walked out to the main office. Greg was busy talking to one of the secretaries. Probably boring her to death about his piece of motoring history, thought Sheila. "Greg, I'll open a bottle of wine for us at my place in about an hour. I need your feedback on all this."

Greg was expecting Sheila's invitation to go over things. He'd worked with her now for just over four years. Their investigative process fell into two very distinct categories. The practical side, the legwork as they often called it, then came the interviews, the gathering of all the relevant information and finally, the all important bit, the creative thinking. All this coupled with experience and, not least of all, a good bottle of wine or two. "Make it a couple of bottles and I'm all yours, Sheila."

"You'll make do with a couple of glasses. I have a feeling this week is going to be one of those weeks for us so I need you on form. Tomorrow morning we're on the eight fifteen to Paddington so get in touch with Richard Harper and his boss Evgeni Berezin and let them know we'll be calling on them tomorrow for a chat. "

Chapter 17

Sergeant Louis Ryan had been at Birmingham Central for over nine years. He'd joined the CID four years ago as a detective constable when Sheila, seeing his potential, recommended his transfer to her department. He'd worked well with the team and was promoted to the rank of sergeant two years previously. Louis Ryan was a good-looking, lively and very ambitious young detective, well liked and respected by his colleagues. He enjoyed the work and had proved himself a very capable and valued member of the team.

Constable Janet Finmore joined CID at about the same time as Sergeant Ryan and had also proved her worth. She was never going to be a contender in any beauty contest. Janet was, however, a very pleasant girl, somewhat plain looking with short, curly, mousy-coloured hair, and a ruddy complexion. Her main aim in life, outside the office, was keeping her weight under control. Five foot three inches tall, she would anxiously check the bathroom scales each morning determined not to exceed the eleven stone mark she managed to get down to a few months earlier. She worked well with Sergeant Ryan who had become to depend on her more and more. Her attention to detail and seemingly tireless examination of evidence gathered by her colleagues had on more than one occasion been a vital ingredient in helping the team to success. These attributes, together with her own very creative ability when searching through possible alternative scenarios in any current investigation, made her a highly valued member at Birmingham Central. This morning she and her sergeant were due to call on Susan Pearce at Raddlebarn Court. Before setting off, however, Sergeant Ryan was interested in his constable's assessment of Miss. Pearce. "When you interviewed Susan Pearce last week you said there were things you felt uneasy about, Janet, things you thought she was holding back on."

"Only a feeling, Louis. I just had the impression she knew more than she was letting on."

"OK, let's just go over a few things." Sergeant Ryan, making space to sit on the side of Janet's desk, opened the folder of statements taken at their investigation of the shooting of Stephen Milligan. "Firstly, Susan Pearce says she heard a car start up at the back of the apartments early Monday morning. She said she heard this when she switched her TV off and went to bed. She knew the time was exactly one o'clock because that's when the film she'd been watching finished."

"That's what she told me," said Janet. "She said she'd just finished watching some movie and was getting ready to go to bed. I even checked the television programmes for Sunday evening and there was a movie which finished at precisely one o'clock Monday morning. It was some old classic on Channel Four called *How to Steal a Million*. It was on from ten forty-five to exactly one o'clock Monday morning. What Susan Pearce told us about hearing a car start up early Monday morning seems to tie up perfectly with the CCTV footage we have of the Audi driving down the Bristol Road at three minutes past one." Sergeant Ryan's attention, thought Janet, is on something else.

"My Dad took me to see that film, *How to Steal a Million*, when I was about eight years old. It was the first time I'd ever been to a cinema. I've seen the movie several times since then. It was my parent's favorite." Constable Finmore was having difficulty showing an interest in her sergeant's reminiscing and was quite relieved when Louis seemed to get back to the investigation. "Now the other thing I've noticed, Janet, is the comment made by Alison Morton, the tenant upstairs in apartment eight, the one next to Stephen's. She said she heard a door slam at about one o'clock. It woke her up apparently. She reckons the door was to one of the apartments downstairs. One of the other tenants, a Martin Harris, commented on Susan's habit of always borrowing things from the other tenants; tea, coffee, sugar, those sorts of things."

Janet couldn't help noticing as Sergeant Ryan was speaking he seemed to be staring out of the office window. His mind's certainly been distracted by something, she thought. It can't be about that movie, surely.

"Right, come on, Janet, let's take a drive over to Raddlebarn Court and see what more Susan Pearce can tell us."

After parking at the rear of Raddlebarn Court, Janet and Louis walked round to the main entrance at the front of the property. Janet rang the buzzer to apartment two which was immediately answered by Susan Pearce who Janet had telephoned before setting out. "It's open, come on through." Walking through the main entrance hall, they passed the stairway then walked over to where Susan Pearce was standing in the doorway of her apartment. "You are the police I take it who telephoned earlier?"

"Yes, Miss. Pearce. I'm Detective Sergeant Ryan and this is Detective Constable Finmore who you've already met."

"Yes, that's right, come in both of you." The layout of Susan's apartment was identical to Stephen Milligan's, the narrow hallway with the lounge on the right, the kitchen at the end of the hall and the bedroom and bathroom on the left. They walked through to the lounge. "Please sit down. Can I get you a coffee or something?"

Sergeant Ryan gave his usual polite answer that they'd not long had something to drink but thanked her for the offer. Susan Pearce, in her forties, rather frail looking, was not exactly what he'd expected. Not unintelligent, he thought, but his first impression was of a woman who'd not exactly achieved a great deal. A rather downbeat one-bedroom apartment, poorly furnished and, unless he was mistaken, a very battered and worn out-looking Ford Fiesta parked outside which he assumed was hers. "Thank you for seeing us, Susan. We wanted to ask you if there was anything else you can remember about the events last weekend, the shooting of Stephen Milligan. Is there anything you can recall about that evening?" Louis thought Susan looked awkward.

"There's nothing more I can tell you. I told everything to your associate last week."

"You said you heard a car start up at the back of the apartments here. Is that correct?"

"Yes, just as I was about to go to bed. I didn't see the car, I heard it start up almost immediately I switched the television off."

"And what time was that, Susan?"

"It was one o'clock, the film I'd been watching finished at one o'clock so I know that was the time. I switched the television off and was about to get ready to go to bed when I heard a car start up and drive off."

"Did you hear anything else? Apparently one of the tenants thought she heard a door closing around about that time. Alison Morton, the tenant who has the apartment next to Stephen's, said she was woken by the sound of a door closing. She thinks it could have been one of the doors down here on the ground floor." Louis noticed Susan was beginning to look more agitated.

"Well I didn't hear anything."

Taking out the photograph of Richard Harper, Louis handed it to Susan. Her reaction was immediate. The look on her face told Ryan she'd seen the man before. "Can you tell me, Susan, have you ever seen this man before?"

Handing the photograph back to Louis, Susan's reply was quick and definite. "No, I've never seen him before."

Louis, just like Constable Finmore, knew she was hiding something. He couldn't be more definite about that. At the moment, though, he was convinced they were not going to get any further with the interview unless perhaps a slightly different angle was used. "Well, that's all we wanted to ask you, Susan. Thank you for your time." As he and Janet got up to walk back to the hallway Louis, very casually began chatting. "What did you think of the movie by the way, *How to Steal a Million*, did you enjoy it?"

Susan looked slightly taken aback, as did Janet. "Yes, it was a good film, I enjoyed watching it."

"One of my parent's favourites," continued Louis as they walked down the hallway. "I thought the twist at the end was good." Susan looked at Louis with an expression which seemed to beg more information. "You know, when they discovered the *Cellini Venus* was in fact genuine not a fake."

"Yes, that surprised me too." Susan's response was quick, perhaps too quick, she realized her mistake. The trap Louis had set had worked.

"Well, thank you for your time, Susan. We may need to speak to you again."

"OK, Louis, are you going to enlighten me or just keep me guessing?" Louis was feeling on top of the world as they drove off from Raddlebarn Court. With a broad grin he turned to Janet.

"You've just witnessed a genius at work, Janet. Firstly, we check things out with Sheila, but my recommendation is, tomorrow, we arrest Susan Pearce on suspicion of perverting the course of justice."

"It's to do with that bloody film isn't it, so come on, are you going to explain to me your 'touch of genius', or just keep me guessing?"

The film, Janet, *How to Steal a Million*., is a classic and, like most movies made in the 1960s, the storyline is simple and straightforward. Movies in those days became successful because of great acting, not special effects and complicated storylines. The story was simple. Nicole Bonnet (played by Audrey Hepburn) had to steal from the Paris Museum a statue called the *Cellini Venus* because it was a fake made by her grandfather. She, with the help of Simon Dermont (played by Peter O'Toole), had to steal the statue from the museum before the insurers could discover it was a fake and not a £1m antique which was the value the insurance company had been asked to place on it. There was no twist at the end. The *Cellini Venus* was a fake and the Bonnet family had to steal it back from the museum before the insurance company found that out. That was the central point of the story. Either Susan Pearce wasn't watching the television that night, or she missed the ending. My question is, if that is correct then, what was she doing? Especially between say twelve thirty and one. Did she go upstairs to borrow something from one of the neighbours as we're told she often did and, if so, did she catch sight of Richard Harper? The only way we're going to find out is to get her in for some serious questioning."

"But why hasn't she said anything? Why would anyone keep something like that to themselves?"

"Probably just scared out of her wits. She certainly comes over as someone who's a bag of nerves, so being a witness to a murder, or knowing she'd actually seen the killer, could have very easily made her clam up. However, whatever the reason, some serious questioning at the station is needed. We'll see what Sheila's thoughts are later."

Chapter 18

.

As Sergeant Ryan and Constable Finmore drove off from Raddlebarn Court, Sheila and Greg were about to disembark from the train they'd caught earlier from New Street Station to Paddington. As reliable as Greg had assured Sheila his piece of motoring history was, she decided a more reliable mode of transport to cover the three hundred and fifty mile or so round trip they'd planned this morning was the better option. After discussing their next move last night, which in the end did require slightly more than the two glasses of wine Sheila attempted to limit them to, the more relaxed journey to the capital was certainly the best choice. This also gave them both time to recap again on events they agreed looked to be uncovering a very complicated side to the killings of Stephen Milligan and Andrew Williams. The discovery her sergeant and Constable Finmore had made yesterday clearly showing a blue Audi estate driving away from Raddlebarn Court minutes after Stephen Milligan was murdered, and the same car recorded driving along the Bristol Road minutes after Billy Spears went missing from the Queen Elizabeth Hospital last year, could surely not just be a coincidence thought Sheila. By a stroke of luck, and not least of all the very diligent work of her officers, her instincts were telling her they may be getting close to uncovering the perpetrator of not only the murders of Stephen Milligan and Andrew Williams, but uncovering the mysterious disappearance of Billy Spears from the Queen Elizabeth Hospital last year. However, the reality of the events coming to light seemed to be uncovering an investigation which had all the makings of something which could easily end up being out of their jurisdiction. That was, as

Sheila saw things, a very real possibility. "OK, Greg, what's the address of this place we're going to?"

"Charter House Villas, Notting Hill. I spoke with Evgeni Berezin's secretary earlier as you know. She was extremely helpful. After checking things out she called back and said both Berezin and Richard Harper would be pleased to help in any enquiry we have, and we could meet up with them at one of Berezin's properties apparently at the moment being used by Richard Harper."

"That all sounds very cordial, Greg, I wonder why they're being so helpful?"

Greg smiled. "Well at least it'll save us having to break the door down, for the moment anyway."

After a twenty minute drive their taxi pulled up outside 37 Charter House Villas. After paying the driver they made their way over to number thirty-seven. Sheila rang the bell. After a short wait the door was opened by a very professional looking, smartly dressed, middle-aged woman. "I take it you are the people I spoke with earlier who wish to speak with Mr. Harper?" Without waiting for a reply the woman opened the door and stood back. "Please come in. I'll advise Mr. Berezin and Richard you're here. Just take a seat over there. I won't be a moment." Not even having the opportunity of introducing themselves, Sheila and Greg sat down on the rather elegant chairs which had been pointed out to them. Looking around the large reception room Sheila was quite taken aback by the very elegant Edwardian architecture of 37 Charter House Villas; the enormous Adam-style fire surround, the high ceilings, the deep ornate coving and ceiling roses, the large gilt-framed mirror over the fireplace and the carefully chosen wall pictures.

Greg whispered, "Now, why aren't we provided with this sort of accommodation, Sheila?"

"And what's wrong with my old apartment I let you stay at, and, I may add, at a knock-down rent?"

Greg gave Sheila one of his cheeky grins. "It's very nice, Sheila, but not quite in this league though."

The smartly dressed woman returned. "Please follow me. Mr. Berezin and Mr. Harper can see you now." Walking from the front reception room down the hallway they where shown into an equally impressive lounge. Enormous patio doors overlooked a small but beautifully arranged rear garden. At the far side of the room stood a tall, smartly dressed gentleman reading through a folder of papers. In his fifties, thought Sheila, and if I'm not mistaken this must be Evgeni Berezin. Removing the horn-rimmed glasses and placing the folder of papers he'd been studying on the side of a coffee table he walked over to them.

"Chief Inspector Whiteman?" then looking at Greg, "and you must be Inspector Williams?" They both shook hands with the man they assumed to be Evgeni Berezin. Again, before Sheila had the opportunity of speaking their host continued. "You wish to have a word with my driver, Richard Harper? He'll be with us in a moment. He's just gone to get some cigarettes for me. One of the many things I've come to enjoy about England, Chief Inspector, the cigarettes. They taste so much better for some reason than the ones you get back home."

Not having been given the opportunity of saying anything since they'd arrived, Sheila was determined now to begin with her questions. "You are, I take it, Evgeni Berezin?"

"Yes, yes, I'm sorry, I haven't properly introduced myself have I? Evgeni Berezin. Now tell me, Chief Inspector, how may we help you?"

"It was actually your driver, Richard Harper, we wished to speak with."

The door to the lounge opened. With a broad grin Evgeni Berezin looked over to the door. "And here he is, Chief Inspector."

Richard Harper, a tall, heavily built guy handed two packs of cigarettes to Evgeni Berezin then turned to Sheila. "You wanted to ask me some questions?" Richard Harper was about what Sheila had envisaged. Well built and what's commonly regarded as 'streetwise'.

"Yes, Richard. On the 21st of June last year you were recorded going through a set of traffic light on the Bristol Road in Edgbaston, Birmingham, at eleven fifteen that night. Can you tell us where you'd been that evening?"

"I'll need to look through my diary, see what deliveries I had, but I go that way at least three or four times a month."

"Three or four times a month, Richard?" Sheila enquired.

"Yes, part of my job is delivering and collecting documents from the medical centers at Birmingham University and the Queen Elizabeth Hospital. Why do you ask?"

"Well, amongst other things we're trying to trace the whereabouts of a Billy Spears who went missing that night from the accident and emergency department at the Queen Elizabeth Hospital. Do either of you happen to know of a Billy Spears or a George McCann who also seems to have disappeared?"

Richard Harper, looking at Evgeni Berezin, shrugged his shoulders. "Never heard of either of them. Why, what's this got to do with me?"

"We're simply making enquiries at the moment. Now, you were also seen driving along the Bristol Road at just after one o'clock last Monday morning. Can you tell us where you'd been that evening?"

"Yes, I remember that one. I was on my back from picking up some documents from the medical center at the Queen Elizabeth Hospital."

"I take it this can be confirmed?"

Richard looked over at Berezin. "Richard, go and get your diary, and bring last year's as well." As Richard made his exit from the room Berezin gave a long, hard look at Sheila. "Chief Inspector, my company is in the business of developing and producing drugs for the treatment of most ailments which blight mankind. We have three laboratories. Two in Warwick, one here in London, as well as a manufacturing complex in Leeds. I employ a team of scientists and medical experts who are constantly working to develop new drugs for the treatment of everything from the simple common cold to searching for ways to help, and hopefully eventually cure, those suffering from alzheimers, cancer, arthritis and a thousand other diseases and ailments. In fact it won't be long, after all the necessary tests have been completed, that we shall be able to offer drugs which will go a long way to cure at least two of the aforementioned ailments." Then with something Sheila could only describe as a cynical smile Berezin looked at her. "But the pharmaceutical industry is a highly competitive business, Chief Inspector. Our competitors would go to any lengths to get hold of details of our research. All our reports, and those forwarded to us by research centers we work with, not only at the Queen Elizabeth but the university in Birmingham amongst many other places, are collected personally by drivers I employ. I'm not happy to trust couriers or indeed any other method of transporting these documents. And, the drivers I employ have to meet a certain criteria. They are chosen because we need people who can not only look after themselves but look after the information they are carrying. I'm sure you understand the point I'm making. You are aware of Richard's background so I hope this answers at least one of your questions."

Richard came back into the lounge carrying two books under his arm. "Last Sunday I'd collected from Birmingham University some documents from a Doctor Morton. Then I popped into see a girlfriend of mine who made me something to eat before my journey back here. I left there at about quarter to one. Turning to the second diary Richard continued. Last year, the 21st of June, when I went through those traffic lights you mentioned on the Bristol Road, I'd been delivering some documents for a Professor Rawlins at the Queen Elizabeth Medical Center. Both Professor Rawlins and Doctor Morton should be able to confirm all this for you." Sheila felt she'd not get anything more from their interview at the moment. After making a note of the information in Richard's diary she thanked Berezin and Harper for their time.

She and Greg walked out of number thirty-seven and along Charter House Villas towards the main High Street. "Did you get the impression all that back there had been well and truly rehearsed, Sheila?"

"Precisely what I was thinking. A bit too well rehearsed. Come on let's get ourselves a sandwich then we'll get back to the office. I'm interested to see what Sergeant Ryan and Constable Finmore might have for us. And get Inspector Goode to check Richard Harper did in fact make a delivery to Professor Rawlins at the Queen Elizabeth Hospital, and Doctor Morton at the university at the times he said he did."

Arriving back at Birmingham Central, Constable Finmore advised Sheila Superintendent Davies wanted a word with her. "Sergeant Ryan is also keen to tell you his suspicions about Susan Pearce. He's convinced she's covering something up about the shooting of Stephen Milligan."

"Right, Constable, I'll have a word with our superintendent first, then you can both update me on your morning's work."

Taking the elevator to the fourth floor Sheila walked over to her superintendent's office. "Come in, Sheila, I need to have a word." Sheila was aware her trip to London to interview Evgeni Berezin and Richard Harper may well have raised a few eyebrows in certain quarters. She'd expected that some sort of 'off the record' chat would be forthcoming. "Your interview with Evgeni Berezin and Richard Harper this morning, Sheila, how did that go?"

"My opinion is it was all well rehearsed, sir. They'd obviously both been advised on how to handle things and how to answer our questions. My feeling is there's one hell of a lot going on behind the façade they put on for us. Hopefully Sergeant Ryan and Constable Finmore may have some answers for us later. As you know we have CCTV footage of Richard Harper driving along the Bristol Road by Raddlebarn Court just minutes after Stephen Milligan was shot last week. Traffic control also have pictures of him skipping the lights on the Bristol Road just ten minutes after Barry Spears went missing from the Queen Elizabeth Hospital."

Superintendent Davies looked thoughtful. Then with raised eyebrows and a look Sheila thought spoke a thousand words said, "You need to tread very carefully, Sheila. I've been advised of a few rumblings from Whitehall over your visit to Evgeni Berezin this morning. He has, as no doubt you are aware, some very influential friends so be very careful and keep me informed as you go along on this one. All this could end up being taken out of our hands, so tread very carefully."

As Sheila took the elevator back to her office she was thinking exactly what she'd expected to happen had just happened. Berezin's knowledge of the workings of the KGB and Russian intelligence was obviously buying him favors and special treatment from more than one source in Whitehall. But just how far would all that go? It probably won't be too long before we discover the answer to that one, she thought.

At five o'clock everyone had assembled for the usual update in the incident room. Sheila, keen to hear what her sergeant and Constable Finmore had found out at Raddlebarn Court asked them for their report. "We called to see Susan Pearce. We didn't stay long but I know she's hiding something. She kept to her story about hearing a car drive off last Monday at one o'clock and confirms her original story that she knew the time because the movie she'd been watching had just finished. But I think she knows a lot more than that. When I made a comment about the movie, it was obvious to me she hadn't been watching it. Either that or she hadn't watched the ending. And when I showed her the photograph of Richard Harper, well, her reaction was obvious. I'm positive she recognized him. One of the tenants upstairs told us Susan was always borrowing things from the other tenants; sugar, tea, coffee, those sort of things. Now, as she obviously had no idea about the ending of the movie she tells us she was watching, I reckon that could be just what she was doing when Stephen Milligan was shot. I don't believe she watched the ending of the film. If, before the movie ended, she went to borrow something from one of the other tenants she could have seen Richard Harper. It ties in not only with her behavior, but the pathologist's report that Stephen Milligan was murdered about twelve thirty to one o'clock. The other thing is, Alison Morton, Stephen's next door neighbour, said she was woken at about one o'clock by a door to one of the apartments on the ground floor slamming shut."

Sheila always knew her sergeant would make a good detective but she needed to remind him of a few things. "There are an awful lot of assumptions in your report, Louis, but, having said that, I like your line of thinking. So what do you think should be our next move?"

"I think we need to get her here and question her again, maybe arrest her under suspicion of perverting the course of justice."

"Right, Sergeant, you and Constable Finmore go and bring her in. I don't think we need to arrest her just yet, but if she shows any resistance then make it clear that's exactly what will happen if she doesn't cooperate." Sheila turned to Greg. "It looks like it's going to be a late night. While we're waiting for Louis to come back with Miss. Pearce, it might be an idea to grab something to eat."

Chapter 19

Their local wasn't busy. Another couple of hours or so and the place will be full, thought Sheila, as she and Greg walked over to the bar. "Remember, nothing alcoholic, Greg. I'll have a coffee and you can forget about anything to eat for me. I'm not hungry at the moment."

A couple of minutes later Greg walked over to the table Sheila had chosen. Placing their coffees on the table he looked out of the window. "It's not raining outside, and it's not cold either so, come on, I need a fag." Reluctantly, Sheila agreed. Sitting on a wooden bench overlooking the small patio garden at the rear of the Jeykll and Hyde Greg lit a cigarette. Just as he was emptying the two packets of sugar into his coffee his mobile rang. "DI Williams. Hi, Louis, how are you getting on? Bloody hell! Well, that'll save us a lot of work. Mind you, thinking about it, it'll probably create a hell of a lot more for us. OK, see you in about twenty minutes." Greg put his mobile back in his pocket. Taking a drag from his cigarette he looked at Sheila. "I don't know what it is about this place but every time we come over here for a break something happens. That was Sergeant Ryan. He's bringing Susan Pearce over to the station now, and guess what? She was about to telephone and tell us she'd seen Richard Harper shoot Stephen Milligan last week but had been too scared to say anything."

Sheila stood up. "Right, come on, let's get back."

"We've got time to finish our coffee first," objected Greg. "And I've only just lit this thing."

"You can get a coffee at the station, and as for those things... It's time you chucked that habit in."

"If my life was a little less stressful, Sheila, I just might be able to do that." Taking a sip of coffee followed by a drag from his cigarette Greg begrudgingly followed Sheila from the garden, through the bar, then out across the road towards the station.

Twenty minutes later Sergeant Ryan and Constable Finmore arrived with Susan Pearce. After escorting her to the interview room they took the elevator to Sheila's office. "Right, Sergeant, I want you and Greg in the interview with me and, Constable, I want you to watch through the screen. I may want your comments afterwards." Taking the elevator down to the ground floor they walked over to the interview rooms. Sheila was thinking to herself how well her sergeant and Constable Finmore had done today. "If this turns out to be the break we need your good work will not go unnoticed," she said. Turning to Sergeant Ryan and Constable Finmore she smiled. "That goes for both of you. Now let's hear what Susan Pearce has to tell us."

Walking into the interview room Sheila noticed how frail Susan Pearce appeared. Switching on the recorder she looked at her. "Susan, this interview is being recorded. The time is seven fifty-five, Tuesday the 22nd of June. I'm Detective Chief Inspector Whiteman, and in the room with us are Detective Inspector Williams and Detective Sergeant Ryan. Now, before we begin you are entitled to legal representation. We can arrange for a solicitor to be present, or you can arrange one yourself if you so wish."

Susan looked pale and very nervous. The dark around her eyes made it obvious she'd not slept much the last week or so, thought Sheila. "No, Chief Inspector, I don't think I need any assistance here. I just want to tell you what happened last Sunday evening which I know I should have done when your officers first called to see me. I was scared you see. I just couldn't think straight." Susan seemed to be struggling to find the right words. "I've been suffering from depression, have done for years now. Probably all my life if the truth is known, but the last twelve months have been absolute hell. I'm having treatment, have been for some while, but I haven't been able to work for over a year now."

Sheila was beginning to feel for Susan. It was obvious she was suffering. She would help her through the interview as carefully as she was able. "If you need a break, Susan, at any time, just say, there's no rush, we just need you to tell us exactly what you know about the events last Sunday evening. Now, you told Sergeant Ryan earlier you were about to call us because you wanted to change your statement. Is that correct?"

"Yes, that's correct. I was watching an old movie last Sunday as I already told your sergeant, but what I didn't say was towards the end of the film I felt unwell. Not unusual for me. Some people call it a sugar drop. Anyway, I felt weak and started to have the shakes. I went and made a cup of tea and found I had no sugar. I went upstairs to see if I could borrow some from Alison in apartment eight."

"What time was this?"

"About twenty to one. Anyway, when I got to the top of the stairs I saw the man in the photograph your officer showed me yesterday. He was standing on the landing outside Stephen Milligan's apartment. He must have just rung the bell because as I was about to go over to Alison's apartment, Stephen's door opened. Then that man standing there took a gun out of his coat pocket and shot him. It took me a few seconds to realize what had just happened. There was no bang as such, no sound of the gun going off, just a sort of thud. Anyway, as he walked into Stephen's apartment I ran back down the stairs back to my apartment."

"Did you slam the door of your apartment, Susan, when you went back inside?"

"No, that was the outer door, the main door to the apartments. I thought afterwards the man upstairs who'd just shot Stephen must have left it propped open for some reason. The wind must have blown it shut. I'm sorry I didn't tell you all this earlier, but I've been so frightened. That and the tablets I've been taking just makes it so hard to think clearly."

"Well, Susan, you've told us now and we're grateful to you for that. There are just a couple of things I need to be absolutely sure of. When the man you saw fired the gun, could you see Stephen Milligan?"

"No, Inspector, I saw him open the door, but then he turned round to go back into his apartment. That's when the man aimed and fired."

"When Stephen opened the door to his apartment did either of them say anything?"

Susan was trying hard to recall the event. "Stephen said something like, 'Oh, it's you again,' something like that."

"And the man who fired the gun, did he say anything?"

"No, I don't think so."

"And you are absolutely sure that was the same man in the photograph Sergeant Ryan showed you earlier?"

"No doubt about that, it was the same man."

"Would you be willing to make a formal identification, Susan?"

"Yes, if you need me to."

"We shall need you to make a formal identification but for the moment I think we can conclude things there. We'll need you to make a written statement, and we'll speak to you again, but for the moment thank you for your assistance. As soon as you've completed your statement I'll arrange for one of our officers to drive you back home."

After arranging a driver to take Susan Pearce back to Raddlebarn Court, Sheila and Greg walked across reception to the elevators. "Right, Greg, I want you and Sergeant Ryan to arrange a warrant for the arrest of Richard Harper on suspicion of the murder of Stephen Milligan. I also want a warrant to search 37 Charter House Villas, and a warrant to impound the car he's been using, the blue Audi estate. We'll also need to arrange some armed backup for us. We need to arrest Richard Harper tonight." Looking at her watch Sheila thought for a second. "We'll aim for about three o' clock this morning. That'll give us time to get everything ready. I said this was going to be a late night, but I was wrong. This is going to turn out to be an early morning, but it looks like we could have the result we're after."

Chapter 20

When Sheila, Greg and Sergeant Ryan arrived at Notting Hill Station, Ladbroke Road, it was two fifteen in the morning. After Greg parked his piece of motoring history he'd persuaded Sheila would be the perfect mode of transport for them they walked over to the station. A large three-storey property built of beige bricks with multi-paneled sash windows which gave the building, thought Sheila, a somewhat theatrical appearance. Walking through to the reception area they were greeted by Inspector Howard who they'd been advised would be in charge of the armed backup they'd requested.

"Chief Inspector, pleased to meet you." Looking over at Greg and Louis, "And this must be Inspector Williams and Detective Sergeant Ryan." After handshakes they followed Inspector Howard through to the meeting room at the rear of the building. Seven armed officers had assembled there all wearing bulletproof vests.

Sheila handed Inspector Howard a folder of papers. "Warrants for the arrest of Richard Harper, the search of 37 Charter House Villas and the impounding of the Audi estate, all in there, Inspector."

"I've had two of my officers keeping an eye on 37 Charter House Villas since we received your request for assistance. It looks like your Mr. Harper was seen going into the property about an hour ago. My officers are keeping a watch on the place so if there's any change to the situation they'll update us." Inspector Howard, pointing to a large noticeboard showing the layout of 37 Charter House Villas, the gardens and surrounding properties continued, "Now, I understand from records that Richard Harper has a bit of a reputation so the best way to approach things is for you, Chief Inspector, and your colleagues to take a back seat. We'll have two officers at the rear of the property." Pointing to the display board Inspector Howard pointed to the two crosses he'd marked. "A further two armed officers will be at the front of the property over here. I don't intend to give anyone the opportunity of resistance so we'll break through the front door. Three of our men will enter there. At the same time two officers will break through the rear door here. Then, with a bit of luck, Mr. Harper will be all yours. Right, everyone, let's get cracking."

Following Inspector Howard and his officers out to the rear courtyard, Sheila was anxious for the apprehension of Richard Harper to be completed. She was now more keen than ever to begin her questioning. She had little doubt he was responsible for the murders of Stephen Milligan and Andrew Williams, but she couldn't help thinking they were embarking upon an investigation here which had the makings of being far more complicated than the norm. What the hell was the motive behind those murders? Sheila was convinced there was a link with the disappearance of George McCann and Billy Spears. If that was so then all that connects to the diamond robbery at Brussels Airport. Tonight, if everything goes to plan, this could be she thought, the beginning of uncovering what lay behind the rather bizarre events it was her task to unravel. But the beginning of what?

Inspector Howard and his officers climbed into the first of the vans parked in the courtyard. Sheila, Greg and Louis climbed into the van parked behind. The constable driving turned to Sheila. "It's only ten minutes to Charter House Villas, ma'am. I'll give our men a couple of minutes then we'll follow." As they drove through Notting Hill Gate their driver looked in his mirror at Sheila. "Two minutes and we'll be there, ma'am." Sure enough, two minutes later they pulled up at Charter House Villas, a few yards from number thirty-seven. Sheila could see Inspector Howard's men about to ram the front door. The rather elegant solid oak door, presented little resistance to their expertize with the battering ram. Three of the armed officers went into the property.

As Sheila alighted from the van she could hear the usual warnings being shouted by the officers, and then, just a couple of minutes later, Inspector Howard came out of the property. As Sheila walked down the road to meet him a number of people had begun to assemble opposite.

Other neighbours were glued to their upstairs windows and a dog was barking somewhere, probably sorry to have missed all the fun, thought Sheila. She walked over to Inspector Howard.

"It's a pathologist you need, Chief Inspector, not armed backup. Richard Harper, if that's who it is in there, is dead. Shot through the head. I've telephoned Doctor Melrose. He'll be here soon."

Sheila had the feeling someone was shadowing the investigation. Or was that just her imagination working overtime. Time will tell, she thought to herself. She walked over to number thirty-seven. "Right I'd better have a look at what we've been left with then."

Inspector Howard almost seemed apologetic. "Our usual contractors, Chief Inspector, will be here in about half an hour to secure the place. Meanwhile, I'll leave three of our officers here. We also have someone coming over to collect the Audi estate." Inspector Howard walked over to the people who'd congregated opposite telling them the show was over. "Sorry about all the noise, ladies and gentlemen, please go back home now. It's all over. There's nothing to see." Sheila, Greg and Louis went into number thirty-seven. The body lying in the hallway between the front reception room and the rear lounge was Richard Harper, no doubt about that. The bullet hole in his forehead was neat. It did not disguise his appearance.

"Right, Louis, you and Greg have a look down here. I'll see what's upstairs."

Sheila walked up the stairway to the center landing. From the landing there were four bedrooms, all doubles. She was beginning to appreciate Greg's comments about the force not offering this sort of accommodation for their officers. "Some hope," she mumbled to herself as she checked each room. There seemed very little in the way of any personal items. The property looked almost unoccupied. She went through the dressers and the cupboards both in the bedrooms and the bathroom but found nothing of interest. Just a few very obvious items in the bathroom, toothbrush, comb, hairbrush, aftershave and a packet of soap tablets. The same in the bedroom Richard had been occupying. Two sets of clothes, suit, jeans, a couple of shirts, but nothing else. No papers or letters apart from his wallet on the bedside cabinet which contained his driving license and seventy pounds in tens, a credit card and Visa card. Sheila went back downstairs. "Anything of interest down here?" she asked as she walked through to the kitchen.

Greg was just finishing looking through the fridge-freezer. "Nothing yet, Sheila, in fact there's hardly anything here. The draws and cupboards are all pretty well empty."

"It's the same upstairs, Greg." Sheila, taking off her plastic gloves, gave one last quick glance round then said, "OK, Greg, we'll get the place thoroughly searched tomorrow and see what forensic might find in the Audi estate Richard's been using. There's little more we can achieve here tonight. Hopefully forensic and the pathologist will have more for us to go on tomorrow. Now you can give us all a ride back to the Midlands in your piece of motoring history."

Leaving the three officers at the house, Sheila, Greg and Louis began the journey back home. It was twenty past five as Greg pulled up outside the property Sheila shared with her partner, John Scarsbrook. "Right, Greg, I'm going to get a shower and a change of clothes, then you can give me a lift to the station. Pick me up at seven."

As Sheila got out of the car Greg remembered something. "Happy Birthday, Sheila. I think you deserve a lie in tomorrow."

Sheila smiled, she'd almost forgotten her birthday. "Thank you, Greg. I think we all deserve a late morning. Make it seven thirty."

"You're all heart, Sheila," replied Greg as he selected first gear.

Greg turned to Louis, "You can kip down on the sofa at mine if you like, but don't get too comfortable. We've only got a couple of hours."

Sheila, searching for the keys in her coat pockets, walked up the pathway to the front door. At the side of the porch was an enormous bouquet of flowers. As she walked a little nearer she could see a card and a bottle of Shiraz. Walking into the hallway she opened the card. It was from John. The message proved yet again how well he knew her.

I asked Steve and Margaret from across the road to leave these for you. Whether you've been working late or starting early, these will be with you for your birthday.
Happy Birthday.

All my love,
John

After taking a shower Sheila slipped on her dressing gown then made herself a coffee. Sitting down on the settee in the lounge she turned the television on and turned the volume to low, just for company. Setting her mobile alarm for seven she relaxed back into the cushions and closed her eyes.

Chapter 21

The buzz of Sheila's mobile alarm woke her at seven o'clock. After taking another shower she began applying her usual make-up. Stopping for a moment she looked in the bathroom mirror. Not too bad, she thought. Maybe just one wrinkle trying to make an appearance on the forehead. I'll have to watch that, but, all in all, not too bad at all, and exactly one year away from the dreaded forty. Sheila put on one of her smart, figure-hugging, two-piece business suits then went down to the kitchen. Two coffees and a piece of toast later the doorbell rang. It was Greg and Louis. "Come in, both of you. I'll make some more coffee."

Both Greg and Louis couldn't help noticing how attractive their chief inspector was looking this morning. Gorgeous figure, long blonde shoulder-length hair, sparkling blue eyes, and after only a couple of hours sleep thought Greg.

Sheila sensed Greg and Louis looking at her. "OK, come on, what is it?"

"Nothing, Sheila, just can't get over how after a mere two hours kip you look as though you've just returned from a couple of weeks break at some health farm. I'm absolutely shattered, and as for Louis, well, he looks like something out of a horror movie."

Sheila smiled. "It's good living that does it, Greg."

"Well that counts me out then."

Pouring three coffees Sheila sat at the dining table. "Help yourself to milk and sugar. I need to sound you out over a few things before we get to the station. We need to talk again with Evgeni Berezin, but before we do we need to do some groundwork. Firstly, did Inspector Goode manage to get in touch with Doctor Morton and Professor Rawlins?"

"He's got an interview with one of them this morning. He was in Manchester yesterday, as you know, trying to track down one of Billy Spears's ex-girlfriends."

"Right, we'll get updated with him later. Now Susan Pearce, I want someone to go over there and check on her. It seems every time we have some sort of breakthrough in this investigation someone else gets there before us, so have someone check on her to make sure she's OK. Then, Louis, I want you to find out absolutely everything you can on Evgeni Berezin, his business, personal life, his apparent fall out with the Russian authorities over that alleged tax fraud, I want to know everything about him. Right, come on, finish your coffees, we've work to do."

Arriving at Birmingham Central, Sheila's first task was to update Superintendent Davies with last night's events. After taking the elevator to the fourth floor she walked across to his office. "Sit down, Sheila. I heard all about your busy night."

"Yes, but as I'm sure you already know someone got to Richard Harper before us."

"Yes, I've heard all about that as well. Now, the statement from Susan Pearce, Sheila, I take it you're happy with that, are you?"

"Yes, I've no doubt her version of events is accurate. I would add, though, Sergeant Ryan and Constable Finmore did a brilliant job uncovering that. It's just a pity someone else took away the opportunity of our getting the full story from Richard Harper."

Superintendent Davies leant back in his chair. "One of the frustrations in this job, Sheila. You think you're getting close to the answers you're after, and then something happens and you find yourself back to square one."

"I know what you mean, sir, but we're not exactly back to square one. At least I don't think so. It just feels more like we've turned off the road we were traveling down. The problem is I'm not exactly sure where all this is leading to." Sheila was thinking things through and turning to Superintendent Davies she began to summarize her thinking. "There's no doubt in my mind Richard Harper murdered Stephen and Andrew, and was behind the disappearance of Billy Spears from the Queen Elizabeth last year. I also believe Evgeni Berezin has the answers we're after. I've got Sergeant Ryan and Constable Finmore going through everything we can find out about Mr. Berezin."

"Well, remember what I told you, Sheila. Evgeni Berezin has some very influential friends so tread very carefully and keep me informed of all progress."

At the main office, Sheila's first task was to complete the report on their attempted arrest of Richard Harper at Charter House Villas. It was eleven o'clock when she'd completed the report. Putting that together with a pile of other papers detailing several unrelated matters at the side of her desk, Sheila muttered, "Over two bloody hours on all this sodding pen-pushing."

As she was about to go and get herself a coffee the phone rang. "Chief Inspector, it's Barbara Platt from forensic. I thought you'd want this information straight away. The Audi estate we've been going over this morning. Under the spare wheel in the boot we've found a .38 caliber pistol and silencer wrapped in a towel. The pathologist confirms it is the gun used in the shooting of Stephen Milligan and Andrew Williams."

"Well, thank you for updating me on that. I appreciate you letting me know so quickly."

"There's something else though, Chief Inspector. I can't give you the details over the phone. Two of our people are on the way over to see you. Are you there for the next hour?"

Sheila thought for a moment. "Yes, I'm here for the next couple of hours, I'll be here." Putting down the receiver Sheila wondered what on earth forensic had come across which they were reluctant to give the details of by telephone.

An hour later Superintendent Davies called Sheila. "I have a couple of people here from forensic. They have some information on that Audi estate you had impounded last night. You'd better get yourself up here straight away."

Two minutes later Sheila walked into her superintendent's office. "These people, Sheila, are from forensic. You already know Doctor Stevens." Superintendent Davies then introduced Sheila to a somewhat bespectacled middle-aged lady. "This is Maureen Watson who I don't believe you've met before."

Sheila walked over to the visitors and after the usual handshakes it was Maureen Watson who began to explain the purpose of their visit. "We have to advise you, Chief Inspector, that traces of chemicals including thallium and polonium-210 have been found on the rear passenger seat of the Audi estate your forensic team have been examining."

Sheila was aware polonium-210 was an extremely toxic and lethal substance. "Wasn't that the substance used, or thought to have been used, to kill some suspected double agent about two years ago?"

Maureen Watson was quick to answer. "That was the substance reportedly used, but it may well have been thallium. However, we'll never know for sure. The files on that incident are buried very deeply under the heading of 'Crimes of State'. Now the fact that it looks as though traces of polonium-210 have been found in the car your forensic team have been examining means we have to report it to the Nuclear anti-Proliferation Agency who will investigate the matter independently. Polonium-210 is, as I'm sure you're aware, not only an absolutely lethal substance but is one of the world's most tightly controlled radioactive isotopes. It happens to be a crucial component in the early stages in the manufacture of nuclear bombs. I've no doubt, Chief Inspector, all of this is probably something which will take precedence over your current investigation, and I'm sorry about that, but as no doubt you'll appreciate the matter is out of our hands." Maureen, opening her handbag, took out a card and handed it to Sheila. "For the moment, Chief Inspector, it'll be best to ask your officers not to broadcast this information, not until all the investigations have been completed. If you need to contact me at any time my office and private numbers are on my card." Maureen and Doctor Stevens, after shaking hands again, left the office.

"Well, that's it, isn't it, sir? There's no way we're going to be able to go any further on this investigation, that's one thing that seems obvious."

Superintendent Davies had the look, thought Sheila, of someone who knew a little more than he'd been letting on. "Not necessarily, Sheila. First of all, I think it would be safe to assume you've uncovered the perpetrator of the shootings of Stephen Milligan and Andrew Williams and, it would appear, Richard Harper was also responsible for the disappearance of Billy Spears from the Queen Elizabeth Hospital last year. Now I've been speaking with the Chief Constable this morning who, it would seem, is very impressed by your work. He's asked that you take over the investigation into the Brussels diamond robbery. Inspector Claes is tied up with other work at the moment, and apart from that it would appear the robbery was not only planned from here, but the diamonds and the perpetrators are over here as well. You'll have the report on the case from the Belgian police first thing in the morning. Now, as I'm sure you won't be too surprised to learn, there is in fact another investigation in process involving Evgeni Berezin. Special Branch have been investigating him for quite a while apparently. It would appear that the shootings of Stephen Milligan and Andrew Williams are connected not only to the diamond robbery but an investigation being carried out on Evgeni Berezin. So the Chief Constable would like you to take over the investigation into the Brussels diamond robbery and share any information you may come across involving Evgeni Berezin with Inspector Houghton from Special Branch. Inspector Houghton is on his way over here now, and will be able to put you in the picture." Looking at his watch Superintendent Davies continued, "He'll be here a little later this afternoon so the first thing you'll need to do is update Inspector Williams, Constable Finmore and Sergeant Ryan with what's happening. The Chief Constable wants you and your team to work, albeit at arms length, with Special Branch. No need to look so down in the mouth, Sheila, it just may be helpful for you to share your ideas with Inspector Houghton."

Sheila took the elevator back to the main office. As she made her way over to her office she beckoned to Greg. "There have been some developments this morning. I'll update you, Sergeant Ryan and Constable Finmore later. Just make sure you're all ready for a meeting at five o'clock."

"OK, Sheila. By the way, you'll never guess who's been seen coming away from Ronnie White's place yesterday."

"No, but I'm sure you're going to tell me."

"Raena McCory. Spotted coming away from his house at ten past three yesterday afternoon before driving back to her apartment at Worcester."

"What the hell is she doing at Ronnie White's place?" Sheila stopped. "Of course! If Franz Zimmerman was behind the diamond robbery, as Inspector Claes believes, then it's possible Raena McCory might have some knowledge of all that. She may even have an idea where the diamonds have been stashed. We know Ronnie White and his crew flew back to England on the 15th of June last year, the day Franz Zimmerman's body was discovered at Broom Hall, but as we are well aware Franz Zimmerman's body wasn't discovered until the afternoon.

Now, Ronnie White was arrested at his home at eleven o'clock that morning so, did he give the diamonds to Billy Spears and George McCann to take over to Broom Hall whilst he went home to deal with things there. Now if Raena McCory is back on the scene and in contact with Ronnie White then it's just possible she might have an idea of where the diamonds have been hidden, or, Ronnie White is hoping she just might be able to point him in the right direction."

Greg interrupted, "But Raena was in Germany on the 14th and 15th of June."

"Yes, Greg, but if Zimmerman had planned the robbery then it's quite possible Miss. McCory may have overheard some of the details when she was working at Broom Hall. She just might have some idea of where Zimmerman planned to stash the diamonds away. Look, Greg, I wasn't going to mention anything until our meeting later, but Special Branch are investigating Evgeni Berezin, and the Chief Constable has not only asked that we take over the investigation into the diamond robbery from Inspector Claes, but we share information with Special Branch along the way. Now, I haven't got all the details yet, but an Inspector Houghton from Special Branch is calling over here this afternoon, so as soon as I've got all the details from him we'll know which way we're going."

Greg, with one of his cheeky smiles looked at Sheila, then, pushing back his shoulders, looked out of the office window. "I think it might be a good idea if I had a word with Miss. McCory, Sheila. This needs, if I may say, the more mature, level-headed approach, don't you think?"

Sheila just managing not to laugh looked at Greg. "When you've finished trying to make me laugh I'll have a coffee. Black, one sugar."

Chapter 22

Inspector Jim Houghton had been with Special Branch for seven years, previously with CID at the Met for just over nine years where he'd achieved the rank of detective inspector. Jim had never really thought of himself as a police officer. If someone had suggested the idea of him joining the force when he was in his teens he'd have laughed at the idea. Jim was often described by his colleagues as somewhat of an anomaly. He was a loner but loved company when it suited him. A defender of law and order, a fighter for justice, but one who was quite happy in breaking all the rules to achieve his goal. His aggressive, creative and sometimes what could only be described as his somewhat dubious methods were ideally suited for the work at Special Branch. He was forty-two years old, married but now seperated, currently living with a girlfriend at an apartment in Streatham. His new lifestyle, for the moment anyway, suited his work schedule and gave him the freedom he desired. His girlfriend, Julia, was happy to allow Jim to come and go as he and his work at Special Branch dictated. His last investigation involved working undercover infiltrating a gang of drug smugglers from Thailand. Narrowly escaping two attempts on his life from an assassin hired to get rid of him, he eventually managed to bring the investigation to a successful conclusion resulting in five members of the gang receiving jail sentences totaling seventy-five years.

Jim was a good-looking guy with a cheeky personality which opened the door to many a young lady's heart and bedroom, both inside and outside his work. Two years ago he'd been given the job to investigate a Russian businessman by the name of Evgeni Berezin and two employees, one at GCHQ the other at MI5, suspected of leaking information to the aforesaid character. The investigation had been both difficult and slow to produce results. There had been more than one occasion when he'd wished for the opportunity of a different case. That was until this morning. Hearing the news of the shooting of Richard Harper just prior to the intended arrest of him by Chief Inspector Whiteman, and the news from forensic confirming traces of thallium and polonium-210 having been found in the car Richard Harper had been using, was the breakthrough his investigation needed. This would, hoped Jim, give the whole investigation a new lease of life. Driving along Smallbrook Queensway he turned into Steelhouse Lane then parked in the multi-story car park above Birmingham Central Police Headquarters. After extinguishing his cigarette Jim picked up his briefcase from the back seat of his car and took the elevator down to the reception area.

The desk sergeant rang Sheila to advise the visitor she'd been expecting had arrived. Two minutes later Jim walked across the general office to meet Sheila. "Inspector Houghton, nice to meet you. I'm DCI Whiteman." Jim was impressed. He'd not only heard all about Sheila's reputation as a DCI, but also how very beautiful this woman was. It was the second of these attributes which was occupying Jim's attention as he took in the beautiful, slim, blonde-haired incredibly sexy woman standing before him. After shaking hands Jim followed Sheila to her office. Sitting opposite her he opened his briefcase, took out a folder of papers and placed them on the desk.

"I heard all about the excitement at Charter House Villas last night," said Jim. "You were right not to go in without armed backup. Just sorry you didn't manage to arrest the bastard."

Sheila was looking at Inspector Houghton thinking to herself how different he appeared from the usual members at Special Branch. A bit of a maverick, she was thinking. I may have to keep him away from Greg otherwise this investigation will end up spending more time in the Jeykll and Hyde than anywhere else. "Yes, we have a reliable witness who saw Richard Harper shoot a Stephen Milligan at his apartment in Birmingham ten days ago. We also believe he was responsible in helping to get out of the Queen Elizabeth Hospital last year a Billy Spears who'd checked himself into the A & E department suffering from some sort of infection."

"Yes, Sheila, I know the story. Billy Spears and George McCann were involved in that diamond robbery at Brussels Airport last year. We're also aware Franz Zimmerman organized it, but the connection with that and Richard Harper, who we've been monitoring for the past couple of years, has come about totally by accident. Now I'm not supposed to reveal details of what I'm working on, Official Secrets Act and all that, but bollocks to that crap. We're going to be working side by side for a while, and from what I've heard about you, Sheila, like me, the only thing we're interested in is getting the result we're after. So let me update you with what I've been involved with, and how I believe our two investigations have come into contact with each other. A couple of years ago we began to investigate Evgeni Berezin. He came to this country some ten years ago after transferring most of his £1 billion fortune to a number of Swiss and British bank accounts. There was some story about him falling out with the Russian authorities over accusations of tax fraud. He always denied any involvement in tax dodging and was more than likely telling the truth, but that was probably the only truthful thing to come out of his mouth since. Berezin has been involved in most things. We know he holds a vast amount of secrets in that head of his. He was for a number of years an advisor to the KGB on security matters. He was also successful in preventing President Putin from expropriating the owners of Yukos, the immensely powerful Russian oil company, from its owners. More recently Berezin has been involved, amongst other activities, in gathering secret business information from his contacts in Moscow and selling this on to London clients. My involvement with this character began a couple of years ago when we became suspicious of his interest in manufacturing chemical and biological substances – chemical weapons to be more precise – and the formula to produce these which we believe he'd sell to anyone who's got the money to purchase them. His business, as you are no doubt aware, develops and manufactures a range of drugs for the pharmaceutical industry. However, we believe one of his many sidelines is the development of chemical and possibly even biological weapons. Now, so far we've been unable to locate where Berezin is developing these chemicals or where he's storing them. There's no connection we can find between Zimmerman and Berezin which is something we originally thought might be the case. They probably knew of each other but there's absolutely nothing to connect them, at least not that we're aware of. Now, my theory is when these characters Billy Spears and

George McCann arrived back here with the diamonds they'd just been successful in nicking from that aircraft at Brussels Airport, their first task was to hide them away somewhere which would be totally secure, somewhere Zimmerman was confident they wouldn't be found. My guess is that place is here, in the Midlands. Now, the theory I have is wherever they've hid them could be the same place Berezin is storing his chemicals. If that's so then Spears and McCann, unbeknown to them, came into contact with these chemicals when stashing the diamonds away. Traces of thallium were found at George McCann's old apartment at Summerfield Avenue, Dudley, and Berezin arranged for that place to be fumigated after his guys got McCann out of there."

"You know that for sure, Jim, that George McCann was poisoned by one of the chemicals Berezin had been concocting?"

"No doubt about that, Shiela."

Sheila continued with her questions. "So Berezin had Billy Spears picked up from the Queen Elizabeth to keep what he'd been contaminated with a secret. Had the doctors found out what he was suffering from then..." Sheila hesitated.

Jim continued his story. "Had they found out he was suffering from one of Berezin's concoctions, Sheila, the shit would have hit the fan for Berezin, and that would have not only cocked-up our investigation, but any chance of our finding out where these things are stored, or where and how they're manufactured. Now this is only a theory of mine but when you think about it, it's logical. Two guys, who we all know were involved in that robbery at Brussels Airport, arrive back in this country with some £90m of uncut diamonds they need to stash away somewhere. A week later they're both infected with thallium or polonium-210, or possibly both of those substances. Now, as way out as all this sounds, the only place they could have come into contact with one, let alone both of those chemicals, is the same place Berezin is storing them. So, Sheila, if you get any idea where those diamonds may have been hidden, let me know. Don't, whatever you do, go near the place. As I've already said, I believe Berezin is manufacturing and storing all this crap right here somewhere, in the Midlands. You only have to see what's been happening in Syria only a couple of weeks ago. The Assad regime used chemical weapons, or so we're told, and the West was on the verge of becoming involved with military action. Now think about it. Whoever used those chemicals was almost successful in creating a second Iraq situation, or worse. Now the Syrian Government are supposed to have agreed for the UN to send inspectors into their country and get rid of their stockpile of chemical weapons. If that happens Berezin could well be asked to supply a new range of chemicals, possibly even more deadly than those the Syrians, and others, already possess. Berezin could sell them the formula, the ingredients and the manufacturing methods. These things pose an even bigger threat than nuclear weapons, and unlike nuclear weapons they're comparatively easy to manufacture once you have the formula and the method to make them. Anyone using them could well ignite the fuse for a nuclear war." For the first time since arriving Sheila noticed a change in the way Jim was looking. A more serious and somewhat deeper expression came over him. "I know we all have to deal with some unpleasant characters, the conmen, the thieves, the killers, but these people I'm trying to put away are beyond all that. They are totally inhuman." Jim almost whispered, "The ones whom the gods will never forgive." Then pulling himself back up in his chair Jim smiled at Sheila. "Anyway, any chance of a coffee?"

Sheila, who'd been engrossed in all Jim had been revealing, got up and went to the main office to ask Constable Finmore to get two coffees sorted for them. Returning to the office she looked at Jim. "Two coffees are on their way."

"I suppose a cigarette is out of the question, Sheila?"

This guy's another Greg, thought Sheila, smiling. Then, looking at her watch, she had an idea. "Tell you what, let's all go across the road. The Jeykll and Hyde is the local we use. I'll introduce you to some other members of my team. I've a feeling you'll get on with our Inspector Williams." Not waiting for the coffees, Sheila, Jim, Constable Finmore and Sergeant Ryan made their way over to the Jeykll and Hyde.

After one glass of house red Sheila decided to call it a day. Sergeant Ryan and Constable Finmore who'd got on very well with Inspector Houghton had just left. Sergeant Ryan had apparently promised to take his girlfriend to some disco in Birmingham, and Constable Finmore just wanted an early night. "Right, Greg, I'll see you and Jim in the morning. We'll have that report from the Brussels Federal Police and we can then decide the way forward." Looking over at Jim who was just about to get another round in, Sheila asked, "You OK for tomorrow, Jim?"

"Yes, Sheila, I should be going back to London tonight but Greg's offered to put me up. I'll be at your office in the morning. And don't look so worried, we'll get a taxi back." As Sheila walked out of the bar her mobile rang. It was a text from John.

Jury returned their verdict this afternoon after just five hours. Not guilty. So on my way home tonight. Get the wine open and we'll go over our plans for the weekend. See you later. xxxx

Sheila was looking forward to the weekend in Paris. I need a break, she thought, especially after today's revelations. Get my batteries recharged, I have a feeling I'm going to need them. Just one more day at the office and we'll be off.

A few miles away at Worcester Apartments, Raena and her friend Christine had also planned a weekend away. Two days at the Grange, Bush Farm. Raena was convinced somewhere there, £90m worth of uncut diamonds had been hidden.

It was seven thirty that evening when John Scarsbrook arrived home. Walking into the hallway he was greeted by Sheila holding two glasses of red wine. "I take it congratulations are in order, John, another not guilty verdict for your latest client." Taking one of the glasses from Sheila John leant forward and kissed her.

"Absolutely right, and just a mere five hours of deliberations is all the jury required. So come on then, what's your week been like?"

Sheila, sitting on the settee next to John, took a sip from her glass. "Colourful is perhaps the word that comes to mind. Colourful and complex. In fact, I wasn't too far away from you yesterday, or more precisely early this morning. Charter House Villas, Notting hill. I thought about calling on you but I was a bit tied up with seven armed officers, a pathologist and a dead body, so I don't think you'd have been too impressed. Not at three o'clock in the morning."

John, smiling, looked at Sheila. "And what on earth were you up to with seven armed officers, a pathologist and a dead body at three o'clock in the morning, or shouldn't I ask?"

"You remember I told you about the shooting of those two nurses the other week. Well, in a round about way that incident is connected to the Brussels diamond theft, but only because, we think, or rather an

Inspector Houghton from Special Branch thinks, they've inadvertently overlapped with one of their investigations. So, John, I'm not only looking forward to our weekend in Paris, but I definitely need the break. Two days in Paris with the love of my life is just what I need. And talking of needs, how about an early night?"

Chapter 23

Seven o'clock the following morning at Worcester Apartments, Raena was woken by the sound of her alarm. Stretching her slim naked body under the quilt she turned over to give Christine a shove. "Come on, Chris, love, we've a lot to do today."

Christine, emerging from under the quilt with squinting eyes, looked at the clock on the bedside cabinet. "It's only seven o'clock," she protested. "There's nothing happening this morning. I'm having a couple more hours kip if you don't mind."

Raena, took no notice of Christine's objections. Standing naked at the side of the bed she looked down at her friend. "Ten minutes, love, and the bathroom is all yours." Walking across the bedroom to the en suite, Raena went through her usual morning routine. Standing under the jets of hot water for a good five minutes she eventually emerged from behind the glass screen. Placing a clean towel on the rail for Christine she wrapped herself in her toweling dressing gown and walked back to the bedroom. "Come on, Chris, I'm going to make some coffee. You've got fifteen minutes to sort yourself out."

As Raena walked out of the bedroom, a grumbling protest preceded Christine's exit from under the quilt. Walking naked across the bedroom she made her way over to the en suite. An hour and several coffees and cigarettes later Raena was going over with her friend their planned two days stay at Bush Farm Holiday Homes. "We can check in any time after midday, Chris. Now, it's only about an hours drive from here so we've got almost three hours yet."

"I wouldn't have minded a couple of those spare hours sleeping."

"Where's your sense of adventure, Chris. This could be the day we dig up £90m or so worth of diamonds." Raena, plugging her laptop in continued, "But there's still something I can't quite get straight in my head."

Christine looked over at her friend. "Lack of sleep can cause you to feel confused, love."

Raena smiled. "It's not lack of sleep, Chris," came the reply as she tapped into her laptop. "There's something that doesn't add up with Domino Mining. Their accounts for the last couple of years don't make sense, and it's bugging me."

"Why, Raena, are you going over those accounts again? We're supposed to be looking for the diamonds Ronnie White and his group nicked from Brussels Airport, not carrying out a financial assessment of Domino Mining."

Raena, with a frown, looked at the information on the screen in front of her. "There's something that's definitely not right here." Then, closing her laptop, Raena shrugged her shoulders. "Something just doesn't add up. My old contact Patrick Dawson at HSBC might have the answers I'm looking for. Hopefully, he'll ring me back later."

Christine, finishing her coffee, got up from the settee. "Come on, Raena, we may as well get some things packed to take with us. You still OK for me to help myself from your wardrobe?"

"No problem, love, help yourself."

At Birmingham Central Sheila had also made an early start to the day. She and John were booked on the five o'clock flight from Birmingham to Paris that afternoon so she was anxious to tie up any loose ends with her team and Inspector Houghton before she left. Sitting round the table in the incident room, Sheila began to update everyone with the changes which had come about with their investigation the previous day. "Right, as you are all aware, Richard Harper, the person we believe was responsible for the shootings of Stephen Milligan and Andrew Williams, was found shot dead before we had the opportunity of arresting him. We also believe Richard Harper was responsible in organizing the disappearance of Billy Spears from the Queen Elizabeth Hospital last year, and the disappearance of George McCann. We know from fingerprint evidence Billy Spears and George McCann took part in the diamond robbery at Brussels Airport last year. The

Chief Constable has now handed that investigation to us. Inspector Claes is tied up apparently with other work and, as it appears the planning of the robbery was carried out here and the diamonds are more than likely stashed away somewhere close by, we now have that investigation all to ourselves. Except, I would add, the possibility that the robbery has inadvertently crossed paths with an investigation Inspector Houghton from Special Branch is currently involved with. So, any relevant information, especially concerning the whereabouts of the diamonds, is to be passed immediately to either myself or Inspector Houghton. Inspector Houghton and Inspector Williams have the details of yesterday's developments and will update you all later. What I would like to do is catch up on a few loose ends regarding our investigation into the shootings of Stephen Milligan and Andrew Williams. Inspector Goode did you manage to speak with Doctor Morton and Professor Rawlins regarding Richard Harper's statement?"

"Yes, I spoke with both of them yesterday. It would appear Richard Harper did call and deliver some documents on the dates he said. However, not at the times he gave. Doctor Morton at the medical center at Birmingham University confirmed Richard Harper delivered some papers to him last week, but not in the evening. It was midday when Richard delivered those items to him. And Professor Rawlins confirmed pretty much the same thing. Richard Harper delivered some papers to him on the 21st of June last year, but not in the evening. It was much earlier in the afternoon."

"How about Billy Spears's ex-girlfriend, any progress tracking her down?"

"Still working on that. Apparently Mrs. Elson, George McCann's ex-landlady, knows her and where she's living now. I don't know yet what the connection is but that's what I've been told. I'm due to call on her next Monday. She's on holiday at the moment, somewhere in Jersey."

"Right, I've had the report this morning from Inspector Claes on their investigation into the diamond robbery. I'm leaving a copy with Inspector Williams. Sergeant Ryan and Constable Finmore, you can leave searching into Evgeni Berezin and start going through this file. Find out everything you can which may be relevant. We'll meet back here first thing Monday morning."

Sheila, driving back home, was now ready for their two-day break in Paris. After packing the last few items she and John made their way to Birmingham Airport.

At Worcester Apartments Raena and Christine had also finished packing a few things to take on their two-day break at Bush Farm Holiday Homes. However, unbeknown to them, Inspector Williams and Inspector Houghton had them both under surveillance.

Chapter 24

After an uneventful hour and twenty minute drive, Raena and Christine arrived at Bush Farm; twelve log cabins set amidst several acres of Cotswold countryside. "I'm impressed, Raena. Looks just as inviting as the pictures on their advertising splurge, which is not usually the case, is it?"

"No, Chris, but we're not here for a holiday. Somewhere hidden here could be £90m of diamonds."

"I still don't know how you think we'll find them. Even if they have been hidden here, how on earth do you think we're are going to have any chance of finding where they're hidden?"

"I hear what you say, Chris, but £90m of diamonds has got to be worth a go, even if it is a long shot. We can look around the place and talk with people who work here. There are bound to be maintenance staff, cleaners, gardeners, someone just may have seen Billy Spears or George McCann. You just never know."

After parking the car, the two girls walked over to the office to check in and collect their keys. The office, a log-built construction, doubled as a shop displaying a range of groceries, books, and newspapers. The woman serving, a large very plumpish lady of around fifty years of age with a somewhat weather-worn face, gave Raena and Christine a welcoming smile. "You must be the couple who booked chalet four."

"Yes, that's right. I'm Raena and this is my friend Christine."

"You're earlier than we expected. I don't think our cleaner has finished getting your chalet ready yet."

"That's no problem, Mrs...?"

"Devonshire, Barbara Devonshire, love." Picking up a set of keys from the board at the back of the counter she handed them to Raena. "You can leave your car where you've parked it. It'll be safe there, and I'll get my husband to bring your cases over in a minute." Pointing across the field Mrs. Devonshire continued, "You're chalet is number four, over there by those trees."

Raena took the keys. "No need to worry about the cases, Barbara, we'll take those, they're not heavy."

"All right, my dears. If there's anything you need you just pop over and ask. My husband, Bernard, will be back in a minute. There's always one of us here. We have a range of groceries, newspapers, some very nice wine as well which I can recommend. If there's anything you need that you can't see here just ask."

Taking the two overnight bags from the boot of her car, Raena handed one to Christine. "Come on then, let's take a look at our chalet." A two minute walk later they arrived at chalet four. Raena noticed the front door was open. As they walked through to the lounge the cleaner Mrs. Devonshire had mentioned was there clearing out the log burner.

"Oh, you must be the new guests. I'm awfully sorry. I was told you'd not be here until tea-time. I'm just finishing getting things ready for you." The woman came over to meet Raena and Christine. "I'm Maureen by the way. I'll not be long now, just want to make sure everything's as it should be. The log burner, by the way, if you want a hand lighting it just say and I'll pop over later. Once they're lit they're dead easy to keep going. There are some logs there at the side of the fireplace and a load more outside, just at the side of the chalet."

Our first contact, thought Raena. I wonder if she could know anything. I'll get talking to her. You never know. "Don't worry too much, Maureen, everything looks perfectly OK to me. Do you fancy a cup of tea or coffee?"

"You know that's the first time in all the years I've been doing this job that anyone has been kind enough to offer me a drink. Usually all I get is just one moan after the other." Maureen suddenly looked a little sheepish, wondering, thought Raena, if she'd gone on too much. Raena was quick to put her mind to rest.

"I know what you mean, Maureen. Before doing the job I do now I used to work in one of the hotels in Birmingham. You know, chambermaid work, cleaning, making sure everything was OK for the guests. And you're right, Maureen, all I ever got was moans and groans." Walking through to the kitchen Raena switched the kettle on. "Coffee or tea?"

"Well that's really nice of you, I'll have coffee if that's OK. White, one sugar please."

"One coffee coming up."

Christine carried their holdalls into the bedroom, smiling to herself as she put them on the bed. The only knowledge Raena has about hotels are the ones you can rent on an hourly basis, she thought. I'll get some mileage out of that with her later.

Returning to the lounge Raena was handing Maureen her coffee. "Aren't you or your friend having one?" enquired Maureen. "No, my sister's diabetic so she has to be very careful what she eats and drinks, and I'm just not thirsty at the moment."

Sister? thought Christine. Diabetic? You just wait, Raena. I think you've lost the plot.

"So you said you've worked here a long time, Maureen?"

"No, not at Bush Farm. I work at the Avon Cross Hotel, about five miles further on along the main road. I'm standing in for the usual cleaner who's on holiday this week. Been at this work for more years than I care to remember, over twenty years now, and I'm still paid less than the minimum wage. But it's convenient, and apart from all my moaning the work is not exactly complicated. I just do everything without thinking now."

A bit like Raena, thought Christine.

"What about the Grange, Maureen, do you know if many people stay there?"

"Apparently, yes. Families in the summer, and Christmas is busy. Then there are the wedding receptions Mr. & Mrs. Devonshire started a few years ago. It hasn't affected the business at the Avon Cross though. We cater for around twenty or so weddings a year up there."

"I bet those events create more work for you, Maureen."

"They certainly do, don't remind me. So what are you and your sister doing here? Just a break for you is it?"

"Well, not exactly. We're journalists and we're doing a feature for one of the TV channels on self-catering holidays, but don't let on will you."

"Oh, no, you can count on me, I won't say a word. So you actually work for one of those holiday programmes on the television?"

"Well, we do the initial groundwork. The article we put together usually starts off going into one of the magazines like *Country Life*, and then, if it's good enough, we're asked to help in preparing a TV documentary."

"So, being journalists you obviously know all about the history of the Grange, and Bush Farm?"

"Not really, Maureen, that's why we're here, to learn what we can. Anything interesting you can tell us could be very helpful."

"You don't know the history of the Grange then, Raena?"

"No, what history is that?"

"Well, during the war the Grange was used by the Ministry of Defence for all sorts of secret work. A bit like Bletchley Park but on a much smaller scale. The Grange used to have tunnels running from the cellar going right under the field next to this one. During the war, apparently, all the top brass used to meet there. Rumor has it even Winston Churchill used to meet his military advisors to discuss things."

Raena wondered if they had just stumbled on where the diamonds had been hidden. Was that possible? "You know Bush Farm could make a feature of that, Maureen. Sightseeing tours of the tunnels used during the war, all that sort of thing. It could be a very lucrative addition for Bush Farm."

"Oh, I don't think so, love, the tunnels haven't been used for decades. They were declared unsafe years ago, and are probably all filled in now anyway." Maureen finishing her coffee stood up. "Now I must stop nattering and get out of your way; let you two settle in."

"If you're here tomorrow, Maureen, pop over. I'd love to have another chat."

"Thank you, Raena, I'll look forward to that, and thank you for the coffee." Raena, looking thoughtful, glanced over at Christine. "What do you make of that then?"

Christine, using her sarcastic voice, was quick to reply. "Well, speaking as your diabetic sister, all I can say is I'm in desperate need of a coffee and a cigarette, that's if I'm allowed to have one in my condition."

Raena laughed. "I was just trying to keep the conversation going with Maureen. I was saying the first thing that came into my head."

"Well it made a change from sex and money, love."

*

Inspector Houghton received an update from his surveillance officer advising him that Raena McCory and her friend Christine Henderson had booked themselves into a place called Bush Farm Holiday Homes, Banbury. After checking through the details of Bush Farm it didn't take long for Jim to realize that this could just be what they'd been looking for. Walking through the main office Jim went over to Greg. "We might just have the break we're after, Greg. Raena McCory and that friend of hers have just booked themselves into a place called Bush Farm Holiday Homes in Banbury. I've just checked the place out and, wait for it, it used to be used by the military as a meeting place for all the top brass. There's almost half a mile of tunnels running from the house there which go under the field adjacent to Bush Farm. When London was coming under increasing attacks during the blitz, several alternative locations were arranged for meetings to take place, and Bush Farm was one of them. When the war was over the government allowed the owners to move back. Then, twenty years ago, they sold out to a Mr. & Mrs. Devonshire who turned the place into a holiday park. It now consists of twelve or so log cabins plus the original property, the Grange, which they also let out for various functions. Now, the Grange has a cellar. That's where the door used to be located leading to the tunnels. Now it doesn't take a bleeding Sherlock Holmes to conclude that could just be the sort of place Berezin and his crew could be hiding, if not working on, their assortment of chemicals."

Greg, pushing back in his chair, looked at Jim. "Why the fucking hell hadn't we, or rather Special Branch been told about this place before? It seems an obvious place to be checked out. Or is that just me oversimplifying the situation?"

"Whatever it is, Greg, I want to get over there and check it out, and I could do with your help. I know this is a Special Branch operation, but fuck that, and anyway, you just might come across those sparklers you and your chief inspector are looking for. So, how do you fancy a bit of undercover work?"

"No problem, Jim, but the drinks will be on you later."

Chapter 25

Telephoning Bush Farm Holiday Park, Greg managed to book a two-day stay at the Grange using the excuse he and his colleague were checking the place out as a possible venue for a conference they'd been asked to organize. Fortunately, as the main holiday rush was coming to an end, Mrs. Devonshire was able to accommodate them. She'd look forward to seeing them both later. As Greg had booked his piece of motoring history, the Ford Lotus Cortina, into the garage for the brakes to be checked over they used Jim's Porsche 911 to drive over to Bush Farm. "Not a bad set of wheels this, Jim, a bit noisy, but not bad."

"Shifts when you want it to, Greg," something Jim was more than happy to demonstrate. Putting his foot on the accelerator he took his pride and joy to over ninety miles an hour within seconds. Then some serious braking was needed so not to completely miss the right hand bend which seemed to have loomed up from nowhere.

"Not bad, Jim, but I still reckon my Lotus Cortina would give you a run for your money."

"We must give it try it one day."

"Whenever you're ready," said Jim.

Greg had a thought, "I'll need to keep a low profile at this holiday park, Jim. I don't want our Miss. McCory seeing me, not yet anyway. She'll recognize me from last year when Inspector Partridge arrested her for bumping off Zimmerman."

"Heard all about that, Greg. Bit of a cock-up wasn't it?"

"You can say that again. It wasn't Inspector Partridge's fault. He was being pushed by those prats at the Home Office who just wanted the whole thing wrapped up asap."

"She's a bit of all right this Miss. McCory from the photos I've seen, Greg."

"Yes, an absolute one-off. She works as a high-class hooker. Nicks information from her wealthy clients with her bugging devices then charges a fortune advising her other clients on investments and business opportunities. She's a slick operator and bloody good at what she does."

"So you reckon Ronnie White has got her to try and find the diamonds he nicked for Zimmerman?"

"It could be. Raena worked at Broom Hall for twelve months, so she just may have information which could help Ronnie. The story goes she managed to get into Broom Hall as a business advisor, but that was to get information on Zimmerman. Her plan, apparently, was to expose him for the right wing fanatic he was. He even had some connection to that bastard in Oslo, Anders Breivik. Anyway, she nicked a painting from Broom Hall we later learnt Zimmerman's father, who was an officer in Hitler's SS, had nicked from Raena's grandparents before shooting them."

"What about Zimmerman? Do you think she did knock him off, Greg, ran that socking big sword through him?"

"I've never been able to make my mind up on that, Jim. She came out, as you know, with a not guilty verdict both for knocking off Zimmerman, and nicking the painting. I personally wouldn't have blamed her if she had bumped him off, but I've never been able to make my mind up on that. I don't think any of us have. I know Sheila has her doubts."

"Great looking woman is Sheila, Greg. I'm tempted to put in for a transfer to your place."

Greg laughed. "Yes, you're right, she is. And a brilliant chief inspector. She also saved me from ruining myself a few years back. I tell you what though, if we wrap this thing up before she gets back we'll never hear the bloody end of it. Likes to be in charge of everything does Sheila."

"Where's she gone to anyway?"

"Paris. Her guy, John Scarsbrook, has taken her there for a couple of days. A birthday present apparently."

"OK, Greg, next on the left and we're there. Look out for the turning." Two minutes later Jim pulled up alongside the reception at Bush Farm.

"You must be the gentlemen who phoned earlier. Two days at the Grange wasn't it?" Barbara Devonshire picked up two sets of keys from the board behind the counter then handed one to Greg. "I'll come over with you and show you both around. I've had the cleaner going over everything, so it should all be ready now. There's rather more to show you at the Grange than the chalets, I'm sure you'll see what an ideal location this would make for your conferences." Walking alongside Barbara, Greg kept himself behind Jim hoping not to be spotted as they made their way over to the Grange.

At chalet four Christine was looking out of the window. "Barbara's just taking two guys over to the Grange, Raena. It looks like they're on their own. We could go over later to introduce ourselves, and then have a look around the place. Maybe find that door in the cellar that's supposed to lead to the tunnels Maureen was on about."

Raena was scanning the scene. "They've turned up in a Porshe 911 so looks like they could be OK for a bob or two. I wonder if they'd like a bit of entertainment tonight."

"Raena, love, don't you ever think of anything else?"

"Only when I'm thinking about all those diamonds, love. Look, Chris, I could keep them busy while you have a good search round the place."

"Raena, two guys on their own? They're more than likely gay anyway."

Raena thought for a second. "No problem, Chris. I prefer you most of the time, but I can always create a good time with someone from the other side, especially two of them together."

"You're unbelievable, Raena." Christine, still smiling, shook her head as she made her way over to the kitchen. "Now, do you want coffee or something stronger? Or perhaps I shouldn't ask that."

Barbara Devonshire began showing her guests around the Grange. "The lounge, the kitchen, the five bedrooms, and finally, the three bathrooms. You could easily accommodate ten people here, you know. And the lounge would make an ideal area to hold your conferences. We could also arrange refreshments for you. We know a very lovely hotel just a few miles up the road if you required extra accommodation for your events. They also have an excellent taxi service. Could be useful to ferry your guests backwards and forwards if that was required."

Greg putting on an impressed look was keen to ask about the cellar. "You have a cellar here as well I understand."

"Yes we have. We normally keep it locked. Health and safety, you know. We have a lot of families staying here. Young kids, they'd be in and out of there like you wouldn't believe if we left it open."

"May we have a look, Barbara? We'd need somewhere for storing our camera, noticeboards and other equipment."

"Yes, come on, I've got the key here." Walking down the large hallway Barbara stopped, then unlocked a somewhat out of place looking wooden door. "It's perfectly dry, but mind the steps as you come down. They're rather steep."

The cellar is very big, thought Greg, and dry as Barbara had said. The walls had numerous wine racks attached to them. "I heard somewhere this was used by the Military of Defence during the war."

"Yes, that's quite correct. There was a door just over there leading to some underground tunnels. Politicians and people from the military needing somewhere safe would meet up here to discuss things apparently. Rumor has it Winston Churchill used the place quite regularly. My husband had to brick the door up years ago when we applied for planning permission to rent the property out."

"Did you or your husband ever go into the tunnels, Barbara?"

"Once when we first purchased the place. We had a brief look down there. Very black and eerie. I was glad when Bernard bricked it up." Barbara, pointing to some brickwork on the far wall, continued, "The door used to be over there. You can see where Bernard bricked it over."

"Well, Barbara, you've been very helpful, and I think there's a good chance you'll have our business. My colleague and I will stay over tonight then make our way back tomorrow. You received our transfer I take it, Barbara?"

"Yes, that's all taken care of. You just enjoy your stay here. If you need anything, you know where we are."

Jim had a thought. "Something to drink wouldn't go amiss, Barbara. I noticed you had a selection of wines at your shop. I'll pop over later and get a couple of bottles."

"No worries. I'll get Maureen to bring them over for you. What's your fancy, red or white?"

Looking over at Greg, Jim asked, "Is red Ok for you, Greg?"

"Red is fine by me."

"Better make it four bottles, Barbara. How much do we owe you?"

"Let me see," said Barbara. "Four bottles, that'll be twenty-five pounds. Tell you what I'll get Maureen to bring an extra bottle, on the house."

Jim handed Barbara the cash. "I'm beginning to take to your holiday farm more and more, Barbara."

"That's what we're here for. I'll make sure your wine is brought over straight away."

Ten minutes later Maureen delivered five bottles of red which Greg and Jim very quickly reduced to four. "I think before we down any more of this stuff we need to have a look at that brickwork Bernard put up. Let's see if we can get through to those tunnels. If Barbara's husband did the work then I reckon it'll only be one brick deep. Looking at the way it's been put up I reckon it wouldn't take much to get through it. A few hefty shoves and it'll probably fall down. But first, you hang on here, Greg, I'm going to get something we might need from the car."

A couple of minutes later Jim returned with a rucksack. Opening it up he took out what looked like a plastic diving suit. Then something Greg did recognize. Two helmets complete with breathing apparatus. "If we do manage to get through to those tunnels then we put these on before we start looking down there. With the sort of shit that just might be there you can't be too careful. Once you've come into contact with some of the concoctions we believe Berezin is cooking up it's too bleeding late. You've had it. Let's have a go at getting through that wall first, then we'll put this gear on."

At chalet four Raena came out of the bedroom in a very skimpy two-piece. "Come on, Chris, it's time we introduced ourselves to the neighbours."

Chapter 26

Greg, coming across some old tools in the cellar, began to chip away at the mortar in the wall Bernard had built covering the entrance to the tunnels. "You were right, Jim, I reckon this won't be difficult to get through. One big shove and the whole lot looks like it'll fall down. By the way, was that the doorbell I just heard?"

"I heard something too. I'll go and have look. You carry on." Jim walked up the steps from the cellar into the hallway and over to the front door. There stood Raena McCory and Christine Henderson.

"Hope you don't mind," said Raena. "Just thought we'd pop over and introduce ourselves. My name's Raena and this is my friend Christine. As we're neighbours we thought we'd come over and say hello."

Jim was trying hard not to laugh. "Well, that's very nice of you both. Come on in, let me get you a drink. My name is Jim, Jim Houghton. Hope you like red, that's all we've got at the moment."

"Red's fine with us," replied Raena, gently nudging Christine over to the settee. "You and your friend on holiday are you?"

"Just checking the place out as a possible venue for a conference our company will be holding later in the year. And what about you two? Holiday is it?" asked Jim as he returned from the kitchen holding a bottle of red and four glasses.

"We're doing an article on self-catering holidays for *Country Life magazine.*"

"That sounds very interesting," said Jim pouring out two glasses of wine for his guests. Handing one to Raena and one to Christine, he poured one for himself and sat down on the settee next to his guests. Greg was right, thought Jim, Raena *is* something very special, and so is her friend sitting next to her.

Wondering how these two would react when they discover who he and Greg really were, and not only that, but at Bush Farm, looking for, amongst other things, the same as they were. Jim's thoughts were interrupted from what, for a split second, he thought sounded like an earthquake. The room seemed to shake from a deep rumbling coming from underneath the lounge floor. Christine, spilling her wine down her blouse jumped up from the settee. "What the hell was that?"

Jim had a pretty good idea. Making his way down the hall he descended the cellar steps, almost falling down in his haste. Through the dust he looked over to where the wall blocking the entrance to the tunnels had been. Both the wall and Greg had gone. The wall had totally collapsed. Jim made his way over to what was now a gaping black hole. He called out, "Greg, are you OK?, Greg?" There was no reply. The lighting in the cellar was not good. He was unable to see anything in the gaping black hole before him. Clambering up the cellar steps he went into the lounge. "Sorry, ladies, my mate's had an accident down there." Taking a flash light from his rucksack Jim dashed back along hallway.

"Shall we call for help?" shouted Raena.

"We might have too. Wait until I can see what's happened first." Jim, almost slipping again on the cellar steps, made his way across the stone floor to the gaping black hole which was once a brick wall. Aiming his flashlight into the abyss, he stared through the cloud of dust still yet to clear. A voice behind him made him turn round.

"Is your mate OK?" It was Raena asking the question.

"I can't see a bloody thing at the moment. All this bleeding dust is making it virtually impossible to see anything."

"Let me have a look." Taking the flashlight from Jim, Raena knelt down on the floor at the edge of the abyss before her and began peering into the darkness. Then, "I can see your friend, look, just over to the left, about ten, twelve feet or so down there."

Jim could see Greg lying on his side. He could then see him beginning to move. "Greg, are you OK? Can you stand up, mate?"

"I'm not sure but I think my arm's broken. It hurts like fuck."

"OK, Greg, you just hang on a second."

Raena grabbed hold of Jim's arm. "Look up there, all that brickwork, that lot's about to fall any minute."

Jim could see this was the opening to the tunnels. Brick walls, floor and ceiling, same design and structure as the sewers, he thought. The problem was the brickwork right above Greg was moving, only very slightly, but it could fall at any minute.

Raena yelled at Chris. "Go and get some sheets off the beds and bring them down here and hurry up." A minute later Chris returned with an armful of sheets. "Right, Jim," said Raena, tying one of the sheets around her waist, "lower me down there then tie another sheet on the end of this one. I'll tie this end round your mate then you can haul him up. And don't forget about me, I'll be next."

Jim looked at Raena. "I can't let you go down there."

"Well if you go there's no fucking way Chris and I could pull you or your mate up, is there?" Without further words Raena slipped herself down to where Greg was just beginning to stand up. Tying the sheet round his waist she looked up at Jim. "OK, he's a big bloke, your mate, so you and Chris start pulling with all you've got." It worked. A minute later Jim, with help from Christine, had managed to haul Greg out of the entrance to the tunnel. Jim threw the sheet down to Raena then hauled her up. "Right, Jim, let's get your mate upstairs. I hope you've got some more wine handy."

Jim smiled. "Thanks, love, you were brilliant."

Raena, with a cheeky grin, winked at Jim. "That's what all the guys say."

Back in the lounge Greg sprawled himself out on the settee. "I'll get an ambulance for you, Greg."

"You won't, Jim, you can pour me a drink though. I don't think my arm's broken, just bruised, and as for calling an ambulance, forget it. I'm OK." Greg looked over at Raena. "Thank you, Raena, and you Christine. If those bricks had fallen I reckon that could have put me out of the running for good. The enormous crash which followed, again from the cellar, was as if the ceiling of bricks had just agreed with Greg. Everyone looked at each other. "And there it goes," said Greg. "Again, thanks."

Christine began to wipe a graze on Greg's forehead with a towel and water. As she cleaned the dust off his face Raena found herself staring at him. "I know you don't I? Fucking hell, you're one of the coppers at Birmingham that nicked me last year."

Greg, smiling, looked at Raena. "Don't worry, love, if you think that's bad enough Jim over there's with Special Branch." Greg started to snigger. Raena, Jim and Christine started laughing. The giggles and laughter carried on for a while.

After a few more glasses of wine, Raena looked at Jim. "OK, you're here for the same thing as we are, aren't you? Come on, cards on the table."

Jim, still trying not to laugh too much, knew he had to be careful with his answers. "Sort of, Raena. Off the record we know you're looking for those diamonds Ronnie White and his crew nicked from Brussels Airport last year, but if they are here you and I both know we can't let you have them. I know I speak for Greg when I say I think you and your friend deserve a handful of them after you're actions this evening, but we're on different sides of the fence unfortunately."

"Haven't either of you ever been tempted?" asked Raena with a cheeky grin. "What would you do, honestly, if you suddenly came across £90m worth of diamonds? Come on, wouldn't you be tempted to keep quiet about it, take early retirement in the Bahamas or somewhere?"

"Actually," said Greg rubbing the bruise on his arm, "that's not a bad idea. Unfortunately, Jim and I have this detective chief inspector at Birmingham called Sheila Whiteman who you met last year when we were investigating Franz Zimmerman's sudden demise."

Raena smiled. "Yes, she's gorgeous, tried to chat her up if you remember, Greg."

"I remember it well, Raena. Anyway, if Jim or I stepped out of line she'd hang us both up by the balls, so we're just going to have to behave ourselves unfortunately."

Jim, pouring everyone a top up from one of the bottles of wine, looked at the other three. "Sometimes the world needs dumb people like Greg and myself. It's not just the diamonds we were hoping may be here somewhere. There's another investigation we're working on. For obvious reasons I can't tell you anything about that, but it's important, and it's one of those situations which need a couple of dumb heads like Greg and I to help sort out. You two, without any thought to your own safety, risked your necks tonight saving Greg. So, if we come across any diamonds, I just may be tempted to put a couple on one side for you."

After what had certainly been an unusual evening, Raena and Christine made their way back to their chalet. As they walked through to the lounge Raena's mobile rang. After a long, somewhat intense conversation, Raena eventually finished the call and put her mobile down. With a broad grin she looked at her friend. "It's time for another holiday, Chris. Have you got your passport with you?"

"It's at your place, why?"

"Because you'll need it tomorrow. We're flying out to Brussels."

"Brussels? What's so special about that place?"

"You'll see, Chris, love, you'll see. I'm not just a pretty face you know."

Christine looked at her friend. What's she cooking up now? she thought. Christine knew that look. Something was going on.

Chapter 27

"They were keen to stay with us, Jim. I reckon we had it made. Crying shame we had to let them go."

"I know, Greg. Anyway, come on, let's have another go at getting into those tunnels. That's if we can get through all that rubble you made down there. For all we know there could be an assortment of very unpleasant concoctions hiding underneath this place. How's your arm by the way? Are you OK to give things another try?"

"Yes, I'll be alright. Hurts like fuck, but it'll be OK."

"It'll be best you stay by the opening anyway. Now, just to be sure, get this on," said Jim handing Greg one of the protective suits. Jim, after demonstrating to Greg how to get into the suits, then went on to explain the breathing apparatus. "The headgear goes on this way round and the air pipe connects here on this filter at the front."

Looking like something out of *Star Wars* the two carefully descended the cellar steps and over to the entrance, or what Jim hoped would be the entrance to the tunnels. The second crash they'd heard earlier had cleared the opening completely. As the dust had settled Jim could see the steps leading down to the brick laid floor of the tunnel. "Right, Greg, you wait here. If you hear a crash just call for backup and don't forget to come and dig me out."

Jim made his way down the steps. Reaching the base of the entrance he began to make his way along the tunnel. After about twenty or thirty meters into the first of the tunnels he was surprised at what good condition they appeared to be in. The brickwork looked in excellent condition. After walking another thirty or so meters Jim could see, about ten meters ahead, a row of metal containers lined up alongside the tunnel wall. They were about five foot in height and two foot in diameter. Looking at them it was obvious they'd been put there very recently. There were twenty containers in all each with a different reference number painted on the top in white paint. Another ten or so meters further on and the tunnel ended by a huge, iron strongroom door, something else, thought Jim, which had been recently put there. It was not dissimilar to the ones used in the strongroom at Barclays Bank where he'd been involved in stopping a couple of terrorists who'd threatened to blow up both themselves and the Ealing branch. Jim made his way back to the cellar. Taking off the protective gear he placed it on the cellar floor. As he and Greg made there way up the cellar stairs, Jim took off the rubber gloves and threw them down on top of the rest of his gear. In the lounge Greg stepped out of his protective suit.

"Did you find what you were looking for, Jim?"

"I'm almost certain of it. Twenty containers recently placed there, all numbered, and a recently fitted strongroom door at the end of the tunnel."

"So the entrance to the tunnel would be about seventy meters or so under the farm adjacent to this place," said Greg.

"Yes, behind the door that's been put there. There's obviously more tunneling leading to an entrance possibly on the other side of the field next to this place. That's someone else's headache though. Our guys will have to go over the layout of the place from archives. Either way, Greg, it's time to call for backup. They'll obviously want the place evacuated before any investigation gets under way, so I'll pop over and warn the girls about what's happening."

Jim made his way over to chalet four. Raena answered the door. "Jim, don't tell me you've found the diamonds?"

"Believe me, love, I wish that's what we had found. I've just popped over to tell you and Chris you may want to make your way back home. This place will be swarming with police who'll want to evacuate the place, so you and Chris might like to make an early exit."

"Evacuate the place Jim? What the hell's going on?"

"I can't tell you that, Raena, I'm afraid, something not very nice though. I wish we were both just looking for diamonds, but sometimes our work is not always as glamorous as diamond robberies. Anyway, I just thought before all the excitement starts you might want to make your way back home."

"OK, Jim, if everyone's going to have to leave then we may as well clear off now. Thanks for letting us know."

"There's just one other thing. Greg will probably want to ask you and Christine some questions in the next few days about Ronnie White and those diamonds. Just tell him what he wants to know. You'll be OK, don't worry."

Leaning forward Raena kissed Jim on the cheek. "No problem, Jim, just don't let him do any more jobs around the house on his own again, OK."

Jim laughed. "Don't worry, I won't."

Jim, on his way back to the Grange, telephoned for backup. The possibility of dangerous chemicals being exposed in the air from the cellars beneath Bush Farm and the adjacent farmland resulted, as Jim had expected, in Bush Farm being evacuated. As the holiday season had almost ended a couple of weeks previously only five of the chalets, including number four, had been occupied that evening. After less than two hours Bush Farm had been evacuated and declared a crime scene. Forensic examiners together with a team of bomb disposal experts, as a precaution, were slowly carrying out their examination of the tunnels. "Greg, I think we've probably outstayed our usefulness here tonight, so let's get back. I've a feeling tomorrow is going to be busy. Your settee still free is it?"

"No problem, Jim. By the way, did you get that message through to your girlfriend?"

"Fucking hell, I knew there was something I hadn't done. I just might need your settee longer than I thought."

Some four hundred and twenty miles south of Banbury, Sheila and John were about to finish their evening meal at the Hotel Bel Ami, Paris. After an hour and twenty minute flight from Birmingham followed by a twenty-five minute taxi ride from Charles de Gaulle Airport, they'd arrived at their hotel earlier that evening. Sheila was impressed with the accommodation, not least of all the bridal suite John had booked for them. "That was without doubt one of the best, if not *the* best, meals I've ever had," said Sheila. "How about we have our coffees in the lounge? I want to have another look at those chandeliers in there."

"I hope you're not getting any ideas for our lounge, Sheila."

"Why not? Something like that would just finish all the refurbishment work we did a couple of years ago."

John smiled. "Sheila, love, we live in an ordinary, although admittedly, quite stylish Edwardian property, but there's no way the lounge could possibly accommodate chandeliers like the ones here."

"I don't mean that big, you plonker," said Sheila smiling. "A bit smaller, maybe, but the same sort of style. They'd look perfect."

John was thinking it would take all his ingenuity to prevent this from happening. "I'll have a word with, Graham, the electrician when we get back. We'd have to be careful not to overload the fuse box."

Sheila could see John was trying hard to avoid her suggestions for illuminating their lounge. I won't upset him, she thought, I'll wait till we get back. John, advising the waiter they'd take coffee in the lounge, walked with Sheila through the dining room over to the main lounge. "So you got the verdict you wanted for your client then?"

"We did, and it was the right one, no doubt about that. However, I'm working on a change to our operations over the next few months. The way forward is for the business to concentrate more on corporate matters rather than criminal work."

"So, John, that'll mean you won't be clearing off to London or wherever quite so often then?"

"Absolutely, you'll have me all to yourself, seven days a week."

"That's good," replied Sheila, "I hate it when you're away."

John, touching Sheila's hand, looked into her eyes. "What would I do without you?"

"We'll need some better lighting in the lounge, though, if you're going to be reading through all those reports you'll be bringing home every night."

John smiled. "I'll have a word with Graham when we get back."

Sheila grabbed John's hand. "Come on, we've got a four-poster bed to try out in that bridal suit you've booked."

Holding hands, they made their way across the reception area to the elevators oblivious to a news item being broadcast on the enormous plasma television screen in the main lobby. The report was about the body of a man, thought to be employed at MI5, being found in his apartment in Pimlico, London, close to the UK's foreign intelligence headquarters. The man, in his mid-thirties, had been discovered wrapped in cling film in the bathroom of his apartment.

Arriving back after their visit to Bush Farm, Raena, in the kitchen of her penthouse apartment, had just finished pouring herself and Christine a glass of wine. As she walked back to the lounge her friend called out. "Raena, you won't believe this! Come in here, quick!"

Walking through to the lounge holding their drinks, Raena saw Christine transfixed to the television screen. "What's so interesting with *Newsnight*, Chris, to get you so excited?"

"That client Kate booked me in with. He's been found dead, wrapped in cling film in his bathroom. He's the one I told you about. You remember? The bloke that supposedly worked with MI5." Putting their drinks on the table at the side of the settee Raena sat down to listen to the report. "The police are saying he died about a week ago," said Christine. "They've confirmed he was working with MI5 in some administrative role, or so they say. He was discovered last week, but for security reasons the story has only just been released."

"Are you sure it's the same guy, Chris?"

"No doubt about it, Raena, and guess what, that's what he got me doing, wrapping him up in cling film. I told you he was a right weirdo. I had nothing to do with what's happened to him, I swear. He was perfectly OK when I left him last week. He even waved me off when I left."

Raena picked up their drinks and handed one to Chris. "Here take a sip of this, love. Of course I know you wouldn't have had anything to do with that. Just calm down a bit."

Christine took a swig of wine and looked at Raena.

"But what the hell's all this about? What on earth have I been caught up in?"

"You haven't been caught up in anything, love. I'll give Kate a ring in the morning; see if she's knows anything. Just stop worrying."

Chapter 28

The garage having completed the work required on Greg's Lotus Cortina had left the car for him at the rear of his apartment the previous day. "You OK to get to the office this morning, Greg?" "I am, thanks, Jim, and I need to get in today and update Louis and Constable Finmore with yesterday's events at Bush Farm. Or should I say non-events as far as our investigation into that diamond robbery is concerned. What's your plan, Jim?"

"I'm off to London. There's been a bit of excitement down there I need updating on. I'll be back later this afternoon. Am I still OK to kip down here for a while longer?"

"Yes, no problem, and don't forget to ring your girlfriend. It's nothing to do with me, but best of luck with all that anyway."

Three cups of coffee and several cigarettes later, Greg and Jim left the apartment. Greg was off to make his way to Birmingham Central, and Jim to start the drive back to London. Driving down the M1 Jim was thinking to himself that, unlike the diamond robbery Greg was involved with, his investigation into Berezin had progressed very quickly the last few days. He was aware his involvement in the investigation would be coming to an end shortly. The work at Special Branch was very different from his previous role as a detective inspector at the Met. The investigations he was carrying through now were very fragmented. No single officer seemed to have charge. You received your instructions, you carried them out and then you were either given a new line of enquiry to follow up or moved to a new investigation.

Jim found driving very relaxing. He often used the time to catch up on his thoughts. There was a lot in the Berezin investigation he was trying to make sense of. The press having now just made public the murder of Colin Maitland at his apartment in Pimlico was, without doubt, going to cause excitement in more than one quarter. Special Branch had been aware of the incident for over a week, but for several reasons the Secret Intelligence Service had been unable to keep it out of the public domain.

The arrest of the employee at GCHQ, Peter Coulson, which he'd also been updated on would, for the time being anyway, be kept secret. The pressure was on for both Special Branch and MI5 to complete their investigations into Berezin before any more revelations became public knowledge. Forensics would shortly be able to confirm their findings on the contents of the containers in the tunnels at Bush Farm, and the latest bit of information he'd received by encoded text confirmed Evgeni Berezin had disappeared. This was something he was not altogether surprised to learn. However, there was one question which had been going round and round Jim's head for several months. Had MI5 been monitoring Berezin, or had they in fact been working with him? Had Colin Maitland and Peter Coulson been set-up? Had they in fact been authorized to pass sensitive information to Berezin? And had the recent accusations that the Assad regime had been using chemical weapons in the war against the rebels been staged so to strengthen the West's argument for not only arming the rebels but to assist them with air strikes? All these possibilities, if true, could be used by many interested parties for their own interests. The other possibility Jim had running through his mind regarded Evgeni Berezin. Had his much publicized fall out with the Russians been staged? Was he in fact working for the Russians to create a situation which could be used to cast a shadow over the West's credibility by making it look like British intelligence was not only aware of his activities here, but actively helping him in his efforts to create an even more deadly assortment of chemical and biological weapons than those which already existed? Jim often reminded himself his work brought him into contact with the very worst of human nature. "The ones whom the gods will never forgive," he'd often say to himself.

Jim couldn't help thinking the investigation into Berezin seemed to have been brought to the surface quite by chance when a gang of diamond robbers came into contact with the chemicals Berezin had been developing when stashing away their haul. But Jim wanted to be sure of that. Had George McCann and Billy Spears stashed the diamonds in the tunnels under Bush Farm? He'd only come across the containers he assumed were the chemicals Berezin had been storing, not any diamonds. If the diamonds had been stashed down there in the tunnels, were they the other side of that metal door? If so, had one of Berezin's men come across them? There were a multitude of questions he wanted answers to. As he approached St James's Park, Westminster, for the meeting with his head of department, he'd at least have two of the answers he was looking for.

DCI Galloway had a vast knowledge of the workings of the British Secret Service. Having spent almost thirty years as an officer at Special Branch he knew more about the workings of both MI5 and MI6 than most. Now just a couple of years away from retirement he was still very much in the forefront of things. Jim Galloway, a big framed guy, some sixteen stone, six foot three, and built like a rock, glanced up at Jim as he entered the office. "We've received some initial reports from forensic about an hour ago, Jim. You'll not be surprised to learn those containers you uncovered at Bush Farm do in fact contain some rather unpleasant concoctions. You did well to find them."

Sliding a folder across the desk he sat back in his chair and looked out of the window of the fifth floor office at New Scotland Yard. Jim read through the report most of which had been blacked out. Details of the chemical substances were far too sensitive a subject to be left open, even for an Inspector of Special Branch. The report by the forensic team at Bush Farm confirmed they'd discovered a highly toxic mix of chemicals in the containers found there. The initial recommendation confirmed Bush Farm would have to remain closed while the safest way to remove the containers had been agreed. It was suggested the tunnels be dismantled piece by piece to ensure no other chemicals were stored there. It was recommended they then be filled in.

Jim's eyes were drawn to a footnote on the report confirming that two boxes of what appeared to be uncut diamonds had been discovered behind some loose bricks in the wall of one of the tunnels opposite the containers. Jim looked over at his chief inspector. "So the diamonds were hidden there then. Well, that, it would seem, puts beyond doubt where George McCann and Billy Spears got infected with Berezin's concoctions."

Galloway, swinging back round in his chair from the window faced Jim. "It looks that way. Let's just hope we're right. The thought that there may be other places where these things are stored doesn't bear thinking about."

"And, Berezin, sir, has gone to ground I understand."

"Possibly, Jim, unless MI5 have him hidden away somewhere. We should know more on that later."

"Colin Maitland and Peter Coulson, sir, any more developments there?"

"Not yet. At the moment I want you to concentrate your efforts on a Christine Henderson and a Kate Summerfield. Now, Christine Henderson is a hooker. She went to entertain Colin Maitland just over a week ago. We now know that Kate Summerfield arranged that liaison. Kate Summerfield works as a madam and she arranged the appointment for Christine Henderson. I want you to check her out; see what you can find. I'm more interested in Kate Summerfield than Christine Henderson. There's a possibility Kate Summerfield could have been working for Berezin. If that is so then it's just possible Berezin could have been aware of how close we were getting to him and began to cover his tracks by eliminating Richard Harper, and then making it look like Colin Maitland died from suffocation during one of his sexual escapades. So, while we have the opportunity of rounding up all of Berezin's cronies, I want Kate Summerfield thoroughly checked out. Our instructions now are to get the whole lot of them out of harms way, clear the whole thing up while we have the chance."

"Kate Summerfield, sir, what do we have on her?"

Sliding another file across the desk, Galloway looked at Jim. "All in there. Get everything you can on her and report back to me." With a wry smile Galloway looked at Jim. "And don't worry too much about Miss. Henderson. She's just an innocent bystander. However, her and her friend, Raena McCory, might be able to give you some information on Kate Summerfield."

Jim was about to reveal his encounter with Raena and Christine yesterday. "Raena McCory and Christine Henderson, sir, ..."

DCI Galloway interrupted him. "I know you and Greg met them last night. Just checking you were going to fill me in on that little detail." Jim, picking up the file on Kate Summerfield, stood up to leave. DCI Galloway swung round in his chair and continued looking out of

154

the window. Without turning round he said, "Don't forget I might be getting close to retirement, but I am always one step ahead of you lot. Concentrate on Kate Summerfield for a while. Let me know when you have anything."

Driving back to Birmingham Jim was wondering how his chief inspector had known about his encounter with Raena and Christine at Bush Farm. It didn't take long to work out. Maureen, he thought. She was on surveillance, not the stand-in cleaner.

Jim pulled into one of the service stations a few miles south of Coventry. After filling up his Porsche 911 with petrol he made his way over to the canteen. Sitting at one of the tables with a burger and coffee he telephoned Greg. "I need to have a chat with Raena and Christine. Do you fancy coming along? And by the way, those diamonds were in the tunnels, behind some bricks apparently. We should have more details on that later." Greg thanked Jim for the update. After confirming Raena's address at Worcester Apartments he said he'd meet him there in about an hour.

Arriving at Worcester Apartments, Greg parked his car in a space behind the apartment block. Five minutes later Jim arrived. "I've telephoned Raena and told her you wanted to have a chat, so they're expecting us." Walking up to the entrance Greg pressed the call button to Raena's apartment. Two minutes later he and Jim were exiting the elevator on the fourth floor. They walked over to the penthouse suite where Raena stood, smiling.

"OK, you've come to tell us you've found them, yes?"

"Sorry, love, not yet, still looking."

"You two aren't much good, are you? Anyway, come in. Do you want a coffee?" Both Greg and Jim agreeing that was a good idea walked through to the lounge. Christine, sprawled out on the sofa, gave a weak sort of smile as they entered

She's looking a bit tense, thought Jim, and I know why. I'll put her out of her misery. "Christine, before we start, I think I know what's going through your head, but you've nothing to worry about. Clive Maitland was bumped off two days after your visit to his apartment. So, being the bearer of that bit of good news, you'll not only be delighted to see us again, but hopefully keen to answer a few questions for me."

Christine was beaming with smiles. "Jim, thanks so much for that. Anything you want, you just ask away."

Raena walked into the lounge with two coffees. "OK, what's going on then? What's Christine offering to do for you without me?"

"That bloke I told you about, Raena, Jim's just told me, they know I had nothing to do with it, he was bumped off two days after I was there."

Raena placed the coffees on the table between the settees. "I told you not to worry, Chris." Raena turned to Greg and Jim. "She's been a right bloody misery since yesterday. We wondered if you might have some information for us on all those goings on down in Pimlico. Certainly get around a bit you two, don't you?" said Raena, flashing one of her cheeky smiles at them. Jim, taking a sip of coffee, looked at Raena.

"I need to ask you both about Kate Summerfield. What can you tell us about her?"

Raena looked at Christine then over to Jim. "She occasionally passes work to us, takes her fee, and the rest is ours. Don't have much to do with her now, not since all the goings on with that bloke from the International Monetary Fund last year. Hardly ever hear from her these days. Anyway, no need. We're busy enough I'm pleased to say."

"But she telephoned you, Christine?" enquired Greg. "Asked you to go and entertain Colin Maitland for a couple of hours?"

"Yes, she did. I was in London at the time so it was no big deal, and the money was good. Bit of a weirdo, though, that bloke. Got me to wrap him in cling film and... Well, all sorts of other weird things."

Raena, smiling, looked at Greg and Jim. "We're going to get Chris to do the cooking at Christmas. She's really handy with the cling film and the baking foil apparently."

Both Jim and Greg with all their years experience in the force had never met anyone quite like the two girls sitting before them. Jim, quickly clearing his head continued.

"OK, Christine, Kate Summerfield, she telephoned you and asked if you were free to go and call on Colin Maitland?"

"That's right."

"How did you get paid?"

"Colin paid me, in cash."

"So Kate Summerfield doesn't make any of the payments directly to you?"

"No, never."

"Do either of you know where we can get in touch with her?"

"I've never actually met her," replied Christine. "All the business is done over the phone."

"I met her once," said Raena. "A couple of years ago at Zimmerman's place, Broom Hall, but that's the only time."

"Can you describe her for me?"

"Well, she's in her forties, good-looking, blonde hair, good figure."

"Did she have an accent at all?"

Raena thought for a moment. "Nothing I can recall, possibly a slight cockney accent, if anything, but I really couldn't be sure."

"Do you have a telephone number for her?"

Raena hesitated for moment then writing down a number on a pad on the coffee table handed it to Jim. "You didn't get this from me, OK?"

"Don't worry, Raena, no one's going to know. Right," said Jim, getting up from the settee, "thank you for the coffee, and your help on all this. Unless you have any questions, Greg, I think that's it. We'll get out of your way."

Greg had noticed something on the coffee table. It was confirmation from a company called ebookers.com confirming two tickets for a flight from Birmingham to Brussels, departure time six forty-five, Sunday morning, from Birmingham International Airport, arriving in Brussels at eight o'clock. "I noticed a suitcase in the hall as we came through. Are you two planning another weekend away again?"

"Brussels for a couple of days, Greg. You two are welcome to join us if you're free."

Greg smiled. "If only, Raena. You two just behave yourselves, OK."

Taking the elevator to the ground floor Greg said, "Brussels, Jim, what on earth are they up to? Why are they off to Brussels?"

"I don't know. Anything those two get up to wouldn't exactly surprise me."

"Brussels, Jim, that could be interesting. Have they've stumbled on something involving those diamonds, and if so, what? We'll get our guy to keep an eye on them for a while longer." Greg had an idea. "Or maybe we should keep an eye on them ourselves for a couple of days. How do you fancy a trip to Brussels?"

Jim shrugged his shoulders. "OK, mate. You gave me a hand at Bush Farm. Maybe it's time I returned the favour."

"I saw their flight confirmation from ebookers.com. Their flight takes off from Birmingham at six forty-five tomorrow morning, and is due to arrive at Brussels at eight o'clock."

"OK, we'll get an earlier flight, then hangout until they arrive. Do a bit of old-fashioned surveillance. This diamond robbery, Greg, is beginning to get quite interesting."

Chapter 29

Back at his apartment Greg booked two tickets for the next flight to Brussels. The only one available before Raena's and Christine's flight was due to take-off at seven o'clock that evening. "We'll need to get a shift on, Jim. When we get to Brussels, though, we'll have about twelve hours before Raena and Christine arrive. The flight I've booked was the only one before tomorrow. Anyway, we'll have some time to take a look around, get ourselves a drink or two, see what the beer's like over there."

Greg, having served in the army before joining the force, had flown pretty much all over Europe. A sergeant in the 2nd Battalion of the Royal Fusiliers he'd served in the Falklands, Cyprus, Germany and Northern Ireland among other places. Jim had also flown on many occasions both in his work at Special Branch and when holidaying abroad. However, unlike Greg, he hated flying. He'd never been able to rid himself of the claustrophobic feelings which came over him every time he stepped into an aircraft.

"You look uncomfortable, Jim."

"Don't like flying, Greg, never have done, never will."

"Don't worry, mate, if anything goes wrong there's only one way down."

"Oh, right, thank you for reminding me."

"Just don't think about it. Tell me what was going on in London this morning. That bloke who's supposed to be with MI5 who was found dead in his apartment wrapped up in cling film. What was all that about?"

"Colin Maitland? We knew he was a bit of a weirdo, but I reckon he'd been set-up. Christine Henderson was lucky. She was asked to visit him as had one or two others of her profession over the past few months. Whoever arranged to bump him off hoped his demise would be blamed on one of his escapades going wrong. What I'd like to know is *who* set him up. We know he was passing information to Berezin as was another guy at GCHQ who's just been arrested. The problem we have though is we can't work out if all this is down to Berezin or our security service, MI5. I'll probably never know for sure. My part in the Berezin investigation will be coming to an end shortly. I'll be moving on to something else very soon. Before that happens I'd like to get a few more answers if only for my own satisfaction. The difference at Special Branch, Greg, is you rarely get to see anything through to completion. You do what you're asked then you get moved on to something else."

"I like to see the results," said Greg. "I'd find it frustrating not knowing how an investigation worked out. I suppose any success with the work you're involved in can't exactly be celebrated down at the local."

"That's one of the downsides," said Jim. "Anyway, I'm intrigued with what's going on with this diamond robbery you've been landed with. I can't at the moment work out what Raena and Christine are up to. There's something going on with those two."

"Well, Jim, we know Franz Zimmerman arranged the robbery, and got his old contact, Ronnie White, to carry it out. We're also working on the assumption that when Ronnie White returned with the diamonds he gave them to George McCann and Billy Spears to take over to Broom Hall while he went home to see what our lot wanted him for. As you know, Ronnie was arrested that morning on a totally unrelated matter and ended up doing another stretch at Wormwood Scrubs. Now, we assume George McCann and Billy Spears, oblivious to the fact Zimmerman had been bumped off the night before, took the diamonds over to Broom Hall to be hidden away as arranged. Sixteen months later, when Ronnie gets released from Wormwood, we know he made contact with Raena to help find where the diamonds had been hidden. He was aware she'd been working with Zimmerman and reckoned she just might know something, maybe have an idea where the diamonds could have been hidden."

"But that doesn't explain what happened when George and Billy got to Broom Hall. We know they didn't meet up with Zimmerman. He was dead, so who met them there and told them to hide the diamonds in those tunnels at Bush Farm? And how did Raena find out that's where they'd been hidden?"

"Well, Raena could have remembered something Zimmerman had mentioned about Bush Farm, put two and two together and decided to have a look around the place. We also believe she might have taken some of Zimmerman's diaries when she nicked that painting from the lounge. If that's the case then maybe she got the information from one of those. The fact is you and I both know the diamonds were hidden at Bush Farm in those tunnels."

"OK, but all that still doesn't tell us why Raena and Christine are flying out to Brussels tomorrow," said Jim

"Like me you don't reckon it's just a couple of days break?"

"No way, Greg, what's there to attract two girls like Raena and Christine?"

Greg was thinking. "Diamonds, Jim. Antwerp is the diamond center of the world and is only twenty-six miles or so from Brussels. However, I very much doubt Raena and Christine, even with all their creative talents, are planning a robbery. No, you're right, Jim, they're on to something, or Raena is. So what is it they know that we don't?"

After landing at Brussels Airport Jim was able to relax. "I need a drink, Greg. Come on, let's find somewhere where we can get a decent drink and kip down for the night."

The waiter on board the *Jeanne Moreau* paused for a moment to admire the stunningly beautiful woman sitting at the table with her partner at the far side of the dining area. The woman was beautiful with long blonde shoulder-length hair, a flawless complexion and deep blue eyes. She wore a white off-the-shoulder Scaasi evening gown which complimented her slim, seductive figure. Around her neck hung a beautiful diamond and emerald necklace. A matching bracelet draped loosely over her right wrist. Expertly uncorking the bottle of Montesquiou Grappe d'or he poured a taster. The woman's partner, taking a sip, nodded with approval. Pouring two full glasses then writing down his customer's choice from the menu the waiter returned to the kitchen.

"This has been a lovely couple of days, John. Thank you so much for such a wonderful and very special birthday present."

"I've enjoyed it as much as you have, Sheila. We'll do it again very soon."

"I'll hold you to that," said Sheila taking another sip of Montesquiou.

"I wonder how everyone at Birmingham Central are getting on without you."

"I hate to think," said Sheila, smiling. "We have one of the Inspectors from Special Branch working with us at the moment. He's a bit of a character, like Greg. What those two have been getting up to I dread to think. Probably spent most of the last couple of days in the Jeykll and Hyde. I'll find out when I get back."

Chapter 30

After booking themselves into the Holiday Inn at Brussels Airport, Jim and Greg spent most of the night in the lounge. With the bar being very conveniently close at hand it was the perfect location. After a few hours sleep followed by coffee and cigarettes, consumed on the balcony of their room to avoid setting off the smoke alarms, they were ready to start their surveillance of Raena and Christine.

It was just five minutes to eight o'clock as they walked over to the arrivals hall. The flight from Birmingham had just landed. Keeping a discreet distance from the gangway used by the incoming passengers Greg and Jim waited.

"I've reserved one of the taxis over there for this morning, Jim. I've paid a retainer, but I'll have to get to a cash machine later and settle up the balance with him."

"OK, Greg, we'll probably need that taxi in a minute. Here come our girls."

Raena was carrying what appeared to be a laptop in her shoulder bag, and Christine had a rather packed-looking *attaché* case. They walked over to the taxi rank and into one of the waiting cabs. Greg and Jim got into the cab they'd reserved. Ten minutes later they pulled up at a place called Boulevard Emile. Raena and Christine, exiting their cab, walked across the main High Street into a large office block. As they disappeared through the enormous glass entrance doors, Greg confirmed with their driver they'd need his services for a while longer. Exiting the cab Jim walked over to the office block. Greg waited by the cab. Three minutes later Jim came out of the office block and walked over to where Greg was standing. "Come on, we'll have a look around that bookshop over the road. We can keep an eye on things from there." An hour later Raena and Christine came out of the office block. On foot, Greg and Jim followed them for about half a mile further into the town. Raena went into another office building while Christine made her way to a coffee house opposite.

Two hours later Raena exited the office block, walked over to the coffee house and joined Christine. They ordered something to eat. An hour later a tall, smartly dressed guy coming from the office block opposite walked over to the coffee house and sat with them. After a few moments he got up from the table and shook hands with Raena. After giving her what looked like a business card he walked back to the offices. Jim quickly followed. Managing to get himself into the same elevator before the doors had closed they went to the fifth floor. The guy Jim was following exited the elevator and walked along the hallway through two double doors clearly displaying RXJ Insurance Assessors & Investigators. Jim made his way back out of the offices and back to where Greg was standing.

A taxi pulled up to collect Raena and Christine. Greg and Jim followed in the taxi they'd reserved. Five minutes later they arrived back at Brussels Airport. Raena and Christine walked through to the departure lounge. Showing his warrant card to the girl at the information desk she confirmed to Jim that Miss. McCory and Miss. Henderson were booked on the three thirty flight to Birmingham.

"They're on their way back to England, Jim. What we have to do now is find out what exactly they've been up to."

"Their first visit, Greg, was to ARG Insurance Company. My guess is that's the insurance company who, a few months ago, paid out £100m to Domino Mining for the diamonds and gold Ronnie White and his crew nicked last year. Their second visit was to a company called RXL Insurance Investigators and Assessors. I think we'll find they are the investigators retained by ARG to check through all the claims made by their policyholders. Now a £100m payout, even for a company the size of ARG, is something they'll not easily push to one side. My guess is their investigation into that claim is still very much ongoing." Jim was becoming more and more intrigued with the investigation. "I'd like to give you a hand tomorrow with all this. That's if your chief inspector doesn't have any objections. She's back in the office tomorrow isn't she?"

"She is, Jim, and I can't see her having any objections. As soon as we get back I'll get Sergeant Ryan and Constable Finmore to check through everything on the robbery, and any details there might be on the payout ARG made to Domino Mining. Ryan and Finmore are pretty good at digging things up. The answers are here somewhere, but they're not obvious. Or are they?"

Chapter 31

Superintendent Davies, taking another sip of coffee, looked across his desk at Sheila. It was just turned seven thirty, Monday morning. "Well, it's the start of another week, Sheila. Did you enjoy your weekend in Paris?"

"I did, thank you, sir. It was certainly what I needed."

"Greg and Jim have been busy while you've been away. As you're aware this diamond robbery has bumped into the investigation Special Branch have been carrying out on Evgeni Berezin. Greg and Inspector Houghton have been working together the last couple of days, but I'll leave them to update you on all that. I know you'll be anxious to get back downstairs to catch up with everything, so we'll have a chat later."

Very understanding this morning was Superintendent Davies, thought Sheila as she took the elevator down to the second floor. Not the usual half-hour lecture. He must have things to do. Walking across the main office she beckoned to Greg and Jim to join her in her office.

"You had a good time in Paris, Sheila?"

"I did, thanks, Greg, and from what Superintendent Davies has just told me it would appear you two have been quite busy. So, come on, what's been happening?"

After detailing the events at Bush Farm on Saturday, and their surveillance of Raena and Christine in Brussels the previous day, Sheila, trying hard not to laugh, sat back in her chair. "I just don't believe you two. And Superintendent Davies, he's aware of all this is he?"

Jim, smiling at Sheila, gave the answer. "We didn't elaborate too much about Greg falling down that hole in the cellar at the Grange, or about Raena jumping in to join him."

"Oh, and by the way, Sheila," said Greg, "Raena sends her regards."

"Does she?" replied Sheila. "Well it appears she risked her life to save yours, Greg. That's something I've no doubt you'll be reminding us about for some time to come."

"Greg and I are trying to work out exactly what Raena and Christine were up to yesterday in Brussels. We've asked Sergeant Ryan and Constable Finmore to dig up everything they can about ARG Insurance and the investigators it appears they have working for them. It appears their investigation into the diamond robbery they had to pay out £100m for is still very much ongoing. The question is, what was Raena and Christine doing calling on them yesterday with a laptop and a rather full-looking *attaché* case?"

Sergeant Ryan put his head round the door. "Have you got a minute? We might have found something which could be of interest." Sergeant Ryan closing the door behind him walked over to Sheila's desk. "We discovered ARG Insurance is offering a £2.5m reward for information leading to the recovery of those diamonds nicked at Brussels Airport last year. Now, there are a few other things which may be of interest. Constable Finmore is putting those together for you now. I'll go and give her a hand. I just thought you might want to know about the reward on offer. That could explain what Raena and her friend were doing in Brussels yesterday."

Greg looked at Jim, then Sheila. "I can't see Raena shopping Ronnie White, can you? Even for £2.5m it just doesn't add up. No, there's something else they're up to, but for the life of me I can't think what that is at the moment."

Sergeant Ryan put his head round the door. "Sorry to bother you again, Sheila, but there's just been a call from Inspector Goode. He's just leaving Mrs. Elson's place. You know, George McCann's old address. Anyway, when he got there an ambulance had been called for the tenant who'd taken over McCann's old apartment. He collapsed this morning after complaining of chronic stomach pains."

Sheila gave Greg and Jim a concerned look. "Sergeant, get forensic to go over and check the place out. We'll have a look later."

A telephone call from the hospital later that morning confirmed the tenant from Mrs. Elson's property, David Walters, had apparently swallowed a piece of glass about a half inch square. Sheila called Jim and Greg to her office.

"Right, we're off to Summerfield Avenue, Dudley. The tenant who's taken over McCann's old apartment has just had a half inch square piece of glass taken out of his gut. According to the doctor I've just spoken with he reckons it looks something like an uncut diamond."

Forty minutes later, Sheila, Greg and Jim arrived at 14 Summerfield Avenue. Exiting Greg's piece of motoring history they walked up the driveway. Sheila rang the bell to Flat 1, Mrs. Elson. "Is there anyone else at your place that would like to call round and pester me?" said Mrs. Elson. She was definitely not amused.

"I'm sorry about all the visits, Mrs. Elson, but we do have a job to do. This is Inspector Williams who you met last time I called, and joining us today is Inspector Houghton. We'd like to have a look around David Walter's flat. I understand our people from forensic are already here."

"Yes, Chief Inspector, they are, so you may as well all join them." Mrs. Elson, taking a step back, held the door open. Sheila, Greg and Jim walked into the hallway and up the stairs to Flat 4.

The large rooms made ideal self-contained units, and were much better than the house share she'd endured as a teenager when studying at Leeds University. There was a large bedsitting area complete with three-quarter size bed, a sitting area with settee, a television, a small table and two chairs. Walking through to the kitchen one of the girls from forensic was in the process of checking the cupboards over the work surface.

"We had a call from the hospital about half an hour ago. The tenant here has swallowed a piece of glass which caused all his problems, apparently. However, you may just as well check everything out while you're here."

Looking round the kitchen Sheila noticed two things which she was sure would explain everything. A half-empty glass of what looked like Coca Cola was on the work surface and, in the corner of the kitchen looking somewhat out of place, a large American-style fridge-freezer. Opening the door of the freezer section Sheila removed the ice box. Emptying the ice cubes into a bowl she held it under the hot tap. A minute later she turned to Greg and Jim. "Just as I thought. George McCann had helped himself to a few of those diamonds for himself, and then hid them here in the ice box. There are eight in here. So it

168

looks as though David pours himself a drink then adds a few chunks of ice. That, it seems, explains what happened." Sheila scooped the eight uncut diamonds off the worktop into a plastic envelope, then sealing it, she turned round to Greg and Jim, smiling. "Well, that's one mystery solved. Come on, let's get back to Birmingham."

Looking at each other Greg and Jim shrugged their shoulders and followed Sheila down the stairs and out to Greg's piece of motoring history.

Chapter 32

Back in her office Sheila was reading through the file on the murder of Franz Zimmerman she'd collected from records earlier. Convinced they'd missed a vital part in their investigation into the diamond robbery she carefully read through the notes made on the 15th of June 2012, and the statements taken on that day. This was the day Franz Zimmerman had been discovered in the lounge of Broom Hall pinned to the back of a chair by a sword which had been thrust through his chest. Jim walked through to her office. Sheila, engrossed in her thoughts, took little notice of Jim's intrusion.

"Ask Greg to join us will you? I think we've been missing the obvious in this investigation." Two minutes later Greg joined them. Sheila pushed the file on the murder of Franz Zimmerman to the side of her desk. "The diamond robbery, the disappearance of George McCann and Billy Spears, and the murders of Andrew Williams and Stephen Milligan haven't just overlapped into the investigation going on into Evgeni Berezin. They're one and the same, albeit with two very different sides." Sheila looked over at Jim. "This wont step on your toes, Jim, or your investigation at Special Branch. You're going to have to trust me on this. Our investigation started with the murders of Stephen Milligan and Andrew Williams. We now know Richard Harper, presumably on instructions from Berezin, was responsible for those killings. Our first thoughts that George McCann and Billy Spears became infected with some toxic substance, when hiding the diamonds away, is now certain. The diamonds, according to Jim, have been found in one of the tunnels at Bush Farm next to those chemicals. We know Franz Zimmerman arranged Ronnie White and his crew to carry out the robbery, but I believe Evgeni Berezin was the brains behind it, not Zimmerman. Berezin, knowing Zimmerman had the contacts with all the expertize to pull off the job, got him to get his guys to carry it out. Berezin must have been aware Zimmerman needed cash, as did Raena McCory. That's how she got into Broom Hall. Her scheme to develop part of the land at the Broom Hall Estate was just what Zimmerman needed, a development promising a quick turnaround with the potential of making several million pounds profit. Now that brings me on to another thought.

"The diamonds were hidden away and I reckon it would have been years before they could be offered for sale. They were, according to the notes on the report from the Domino Mining Corporation, of a unique colouring. So even after two or three years they'd have had to have been sold very slowly, almost one by one if the information I've been going through is correct. If all that is so then it would have taken several years to get rid of them. I don't think Zimmerman could have afforded to wait that long. I think he'd more than likely done some sort of deal with Berezin, a one-off payment, perhaps, on delivery of the diamonds. Now that makes more sense to me than the assumption George McCann and Billy Spears, simply by chance, happened to hide the diamonds in the same place Berezin was storing his chemicals." Getting up from her desk Sheila picked up her mobile and turned to Greg and Jim. "Come on, you two. There are two people who may just be able to help back this up. Bernard and Barbara Zimmerman, they moved to a place in Warwick last year. I've got the address. Greg, you can drive."

Chapter 33

Using Greg's piece of motoring history, Sheila, Greg and Jim arrived at the property Bernard and Barbara had moved to after vacating their cottage on the Broom Hall Estate the previous year. The rather modest, two-bedroom terraced property was situated on the outskirts of Warwick in a cul-de-sac just off the main Warwick Road. Greg pulled up outside. "Come down a bit in the world haven't they, Sheila?"

"Yes, Greg. Zimmerman's estate is still tied up in probate at the moment. The Inland Revenue are, from what I've been told, going through things with a fine-tooth comb, and it's rumored Franz Zimmerman ended up virtually bankrupt. Anyway, come on, let's see what Bernard and Sylvia can tell us."

It was Bernard Zimmerman who answered the door. With a somewhat surprised and rather disappointing look he invited Sheila and her two officers into the front room of his new home. "Thank you for seeing us, Bernard. I'm sorry to have to drag up all the events at Broom Hall last year which no doubt you'd rather forget about, but I'm hoping you may be able to answer a few questions for me." Bernard, inviting Sheila, Greg and Jim to take a seat at the small dining table set in the bay window of the front room, sat down opposite them. "Bernard, in your statement taken on the 15th of June last year, the day your father was discovered in the lounge of Broom Hall, you stated you saw a number of people arriving at the hall that morning. Is that correct?"

"Yes, Chief Inspector, there were always people coming and going at the hall."

"According to my notes, Bernard, it was your father's secretary and housekeeper's day off, so I assume anyone calling would not have gained access that morning?"

"That's correct. My father's secretary, Miss. Peters, didn't arrive till later that afternoon. It was her, if you recall, who discovered my father's body."

"Did any of the visitors that morning happen to call over to your cottage?"

"No, we had no visitors."

A woman's voice made Sheila turn round. Barbara Zimmerman, closing the door behind her, came over to the table and sat down next to her husband.

"Why don't you just tell the Inspector what she wants to know? Don't you think it's time we all stopped covering up for you father? Hasn't he caused enough damage and heartache?" Barbara, looking at Sheila, enquired, "How can we help you, Chief Inspector?"

Sheila, taking the photographs of George McCann, Billy Spears and Richard Harper from the folder she was holding, handed them to Barbara Zimmerman. "On the morning Franz Zimmerman was found at Broom Hall did either of you see any of these gentlemen at or near the hall?"

Barbara looked at the photocopies Sheila handed to her. "Yes, that one." Pointing to the picture of Richard Harper, Barbara handed the photocopies back to Sheila. "That's Richard Harper. He called at the hall a few times last year. He works for one of Franz Zimmerman's business associates who also used to call there. Russian guy, funny name, Berzin, or something like that."

"Evgeni Berezin?" enquired Sheila.

"Yes, that's it, he introduced me to him once. It was the housekeeper's day off and Bernard's Dad had me making the coffee and refreshments for them at one of their meetings. I thought he was all right until I heard them arguing once. For a Russian he certainly had a grasp of the English language, especially the four-letter variety. He was shouting at Zimmerman telling him the deal was £5m on delivery, and if he tried to double-cross him it would be the last thing he ever did."

"When was this, Barbara?"

"About a month before he was murdered, Chief Inspector."

"And you didn't think it important to mention this to us during our investigation?"

"No, Chief Inspector, I didn't think it important. People were always threatening Franz Zimmerman about one thing or another. I told you on your first visit to us that he probably had more people wishing him harm than I could count. The sort of argument I've just described happened on a regular basis at Broom Hall."

"And you don't remember seeing either of the other two in these photographs?"

"No, Chief Inspector, I don't think I've seen either of them before."

"They were there as well, Chief Inspector," said Bernard, "at the hall, the day my father's body was found."

Bernard had obviously, thought Sheila, decided to take his wife's advice and answer her questions.

"So, Bernard, you're saying Richard Harper and the other two in this photograph were at Broom Hall on the morning of the 15th of June last year?"

"Yes, Chief Inspector. I'd gone over to the main entrance at the side of the hall to meet who I thought were the contractors my father had arranged to call to give an estimate for resurfacing the driveways. I couldn't quite see from our cottage who it was standing outside the hall. They had their backs to me. When I got over there I saw it was Richard Harper. The other two I'd never seen before."

"Did you hear anything they were saying, Bernard?"

"One of the guys said something about the police being at Ronnie's place so he'd been told to make the delivery. Richard handed a piece of paper to one of them. The next thing I couldn't help but notice was the speed Richard Harper drove off."

"And the other two, Bernard?"

"They drove off a few minutes later in the opposite direction, if that's of any interest to you."

Picking up her file of papers Sheila got up from the table. "You've both been very helpful. We may need to speak to you again, but for the moment we'll get out of your way."

Sheila was now convinced how the two investigations were connected. Her theory was very quickly gaining substance. However, the main perpetrators were either dead or out of her jurisdiction, but that was not going to stop her putting together what she was now convinced were the series of events connecting Franz Zimmerman, Evgeni Berezin, Ronnie White and the murders of Stephen Milligan and Andrew Williams to the Brussels diamond robbery. It also told her who, almost without question, was responsible for the murder of Franz Zimmerman last year. She'd always doubted Raena McCory had murdered Zimmerman. Now, it seemed, those doubts had been confirmed.

Back at Birmingham Sheila called Greg and Jim to her office. "I think we can start to put a few things together, at least from our side of the investigation. It may even help with your team at Special Branch, Jim."

"It may do, Sheila, but I'll probably be moving on to something else very soon. I was telling Greg the other day you rarely see anything through with the work we do down there. Just the way the things are handled. It can be a bit frustrating at times." Jim looked at Sheila and began to summarize his thoughts. "That aside what we've had confirmed this morning tells us who bumped Zimmerman off, and why. Maybe Berezin had a falling out with Zimmerman over payment. Berezin sends Richard Harper round to Broom Hall, he sticks that sword through him then waits for Ronnie White to turn up the next morning as arranged. When McCann and Spears turn up and tell him they're there because the police are at Ronnie White's place, literally fifteen minutes drive away, Richard Harper can't wait to make himself scarce. He gives McCann and Spears the address of Bush Farm and tells them where the entrance is to the tunnels at the other side of the field. He then makes himself scarce. Later when Berezin learns McCann and Spears have been infected with his concoctions he gets Richard Harper to go and make sure they're out of harms way, so to speak. That explains why Richard Harper didn't take the diamonds from McCann and Spears, and take them over to Bush Farm himself. He'd obviously thought the visit by the police at Ronnie White's place was to do with the robbery in Brussels. He was worried the whole thing had been rumbled. He wasn't going to hang about to explain £90m worth of diamonds and a very dead Franz Zimmerman in the lounge of Broom Hall with a socking big sword pinning him to the back of the chair he was sitting in."

"I have a question, Jim. That strongroom door you saw in the tunnels by the containers. If the entrance to the tunnels is the other side of the field next to Bush Farm then how did McCann and Spears get through that? The diamonds were found opposite the containers weren't they?"

"Yes, Greg, but that door had only just been fitted. The brickwork surrounding it was new. The door had recently been fitted. It probably wasn't there last year." Jim, beginning to pace up and down Sheila's office, looked at Sheila then Greg. "Now, I have a question. What are Raena and Christine up to? We've learnt a lot this morning, but I think there's a hell of a lot more behind all this. Unless I'm very much mistaken, Raena has the answers. But what the hell does she know that we don't?"

Chapter 34

At Worcester Apartments Raena had spent almost the whole morning in the kitchen making calls on her mobile. Walking down the hallway of her penthouse suite she walked through to the lounge. Looking over at Christine who lay slumped on the settee wearing nothing but a T-shirt she thought to herself just how beautiful she looked. "I'll marry you one day, love."

Christine laughed. "Well that'll get the neighbours talking, Raena."

"OK, Chris, love, get your knickers on. We're on the three thirty flight to Brussels this afternoon."

"Brussels, Raena? Again? What for this time? I really need to get back and earn some money otherwise you'll have to marry me and start giving me an allowance."

"Your money worries may just be coming to an end, Chris. So come on, get something out of my wardrobe to wear. Our taxi for the airport will be here in an hour."

Superintendent Davies had some news for Sheila. Taking the elevator to the second floor he walked over to her office. Having half an hour before his lunch appointment with the Assistant Chief Constable he'd decided to take the opportunity to update Sheila on a couple of matters. "This is an unexpected visit, sir, not in trouble down here are we?"

Superintendent Davies, smiling, looked across the desk at his chief inspector. "No, Sheila, but I do want to update you about a chat I had this morning with DI Goode. He's been offered a position at Leicester. William Maynard, the superintendent there, will be retiring next year, and DI Goode, who we are all aware is the ambitious type, feels he'd have more chance of promotion there. So, he'll be moving over to Leicester next month. He'll be popping in to see you later so I thought I'd update you on what's happening."

"Well, thank you for letting me know, sir. I have to say DI Goode and I got on a lot better than I originally thought we would. He's a good DI, and hard-working. I wish him every success."

"We'll need to sort out a replacement, Sheila, so if you've any ideas let me know." Looking at his watch Superintendent Davies got up from his chair. "Now I must go, I have a lunch appointment with the Assistant Chief Constable."

"Well enjoy your lunch, sir," said Sheila as her superintendent left the office.

I think I'll indulge in a sandwich and a coffee, thought Sheila. It's a beautiful summers day, so why not? Looking across the office Sheila was wondering if Greg and Jim may like to join her at the Jekyll and Hyde. Walking over to the elevator she beckoned to Greg. "Just popping over the road, Greg, do you fancy a break for ten minutes?"

"Count me in, Sheila," said Greg grabbing his jacket.

"Any sign of Jim?" said Sheila.

Across the office Greg saw Jim exiting the elevator. "He looks deep in thought again, Sheila."

Greg walked over to him and said they were popping over to the Jekyll and Hyde if he fancied a coffee.

"I've just got one call to make, Greg, I'll be over in a couple of minutes."

As Sheila and Greg were making their way across the road for a coffee break forensic were trying to contact Sheila. There had been some rather surprising developments which they were keen to update her on. They asked the desk sergeant to get her to ring them back immediately upon her return. Superintendent Galloway at Special Branch was already explaining to Jim what forensic had discovered.

At the Jekyll and Hyde Greg ordered two coffees at the bar. Sheila seemed more concerned with her figure after eating so much in Paris at the weekend to be tempted by the sandwiches on offer, and Greg just wanted a cigarette with his coffee. They found a table in the gardens. "What a beautiful day, Sheila," remarked Greg as he lit his Marlboro King Size. "You know, every time we come over here something happens, and we end up dashing back over the road. Well, not today," said Greg. "We've done well, you know. We not only know who was responsible for shooting Stephen and Andrew, but it looks like we've identified who shoved that socking big sword through Franz Zimmerman last year."

"The diamond robbery though, Greg, that's something we've yet to get to grips with. We know Ronnie White and his crew carried it out, but how we're going to get enough to prove that I'm not sure yet. And by the way, Superintendent Davies informed me this morning Inspector Goode is transferring to Leicester. He'll be leaving us next month so we'll need a replacement."

"Well that's something you've got to deal with, Sheila. He wasn't that bad a bloke you know. I got on with him quite well. A bit formal, but he was OK. Anyway, I wish him luck." Greg, taking another sip of coffee, sat back and enjoyed another drag from his Marlboro.

"I thought this is where I'd find you both."

A voice behind him made Greg turn round. It was Jim. Lighting up a cigarette he looked at Greg and then at Sheila. "I don't know whether to tell you this, Sheila, until we've finished our fags, but provided you promise to give us both ten minutes before you make us dash back over the road I'll tell you."

"If you have something to tell me, Inspector, get on with it."

"The diamonds, Sheila, they're not diamonds. They're just pieces of worthless molten glass, every one of them. Including the one cut out of David Walter's stomach yesterday."

No one said a word. At least, thought Greg, I may be able to finish my fag.

Chapter 35

It was six fifteen that evening as flight number KL1424 from Birmingham touched down at Brussels Airport. A few moments later Raena and Christine, complete with *attaché* case, laptop and overnight bag, walked through the arrivals lounge and over to the Holiday Inn Hotel. Christine felt determined this time to get Raena to explain what they were supposed to be doing. "Come on, Raena, I've had enough of all this. Are you going to tell me what the hell we're doing over here again?"

"In a couple of hours time, Chris, love, we'll be on the next flight back to Birmingham with enough money to stop you moaning ever again. Now get me a drink and I'll explain." Returning with their drinks Christine placed the two glasses of white house wine on the table.

"OK, come on then, Raena, what are we doing here, and more importantly where's all that money you said we would be going home with coming from?"

"ARG Insurance, Chris, the company who paid out the £100m to the Domino Mining Corporation. They've been offering a £2.5m reward leading to the return of the diamonds Ronnie and his crew nicked from Brussels Airport last year. I've been able to negotiate an increase in that to £6m. That's £2m each. You, me and Ronnie, £2m each."

"But, Raena, love, just a small detail. We don't know where the fuck the diamonds have been hidden."

Raena smiled. "You have such a lovely way with words, Chris. There are no diamonds, there never was. When I was at Broom Hall, I learnt that Franz Zimmerman had been planning a robbery with

180

Alan Alexander, the Chief Executive of Domino Mining, who took over there a couple of years ago. Now, for various reasons their plans were put on hold partly due to the difficulty in arranging for the security company to keep well out of the way on the day. Anyway, when things had been worked out, Ronnie White, who Zimmerman had outlined his plans to eighteen months previously had, as luck would have it, just been released from Wormwood Scrubs. So, he and his crew got ready to carry out what everyone thought was to be the biggest robbery ever.

"Now, when I went over the accounts for Domino Mining it was obvious the company was on the verge of bankruptcy and had been since two disastrous and very costly errors were made when the company decided to purchase a new mining enterprise in Zimbabwe. Anyway, I'll skip the details on that. The fact remained the company last year was about to be issued with a winding-up order. Now the Chief Executive, Alan Alexander, who'd been brought in a couple of years previously to turn the company round, was determined to succeed. One of those guys who'd never let anything get in his way. He knew Franz Zimmerman and, between them, they cooked up a scheme to nick £100m worth of the company's diamonds on their way from Antwerp to Zurich. The plan was by substituting the diamonds for pieces of molten glass they'd claim the insurance monies and still have the diamonds. However, by March 2012 the situation for both Domino Mining and Franz Zimmerman had deteriorated to the point where both of them were on the verge of bankruptcy. Zimmerman knew there was no way he could wait several years for any payout from the robbery, and Alan Alexander was determined not only to save Domino Mining from going under, but to complete his plans to purchase another company, Kingstone Mining, which he'd had his eye on for some years. This company would compliment the way Domino Mining operated, and had the potential of turning round the company's fortunes very quickly. Zimmerman, however, desperate for money, got in touch with Evgeni Berezin who he'd done business with before, and strikes a deal to sell the diamonds at some knock-down price as soon as Ronnie had made delivery. It's obvious from the balance sheets and conversations I've had with two of my contacts at HSBC that Zimmerman was not the only one who couldn't afford to wait for a payout. Domino Mining also needed the money, in fact, immediately. Anyway, the records show that Domino

Mining made a payment in June, less than two weeks after the robbery had been carried out, and cleared a debt of £34m with the company about to issue proceedings to have them wound up. That transaction was never recorded on their balance sheets. It was obvious Domino Mining had paid that debt using uncut diamonds. Then a few months later they signed contracts to purchase Kingstone Mining and paid £50m towards the purchase price of £150m. Again, this payment hadn't appeared on the company balance sheets. This payment, as well, had obviously been made with uncut diamonds. The balance of £100m was paid two weeks after ARG settled the insurance claim. Neither the deposit of £50m or the payment of £34m to one of their creditors had been paid through any bank. It couldn't have been. Domino Mining hadn't the cash, and no bank would have been willing to lend to a company they believed had no chance of surviving. Both these payments had been made using uncut diamonds at, no doubt, a discounted price.

"Now, as for Franz Zimmerman, at the end of the day, Chris, it was poetic justice for him. He'd finally met two people who turned out to be even bigger bastards than he was. Alan Alexander, who double-crossed him by swopping the diamonds for worthless pieces of glass, and Evgeni Berezin who had Zimmerman bumped off when he attempted to negotiate a higher price. I told you I wasn't just a pretty face, Chris."

That's something I'm sure you'll remind me again and again, thought Christine, sipping her wine. "So what happens now, Raena?"

"We're meeting up here with the two guys from ARG Insurance I spoke with on our last visit. As soon as they've signed the agreement I left with them I'll then explain exactly where the diamonds they paid £100m for are hidden, or at least what happened to them. They'll then be able to get their money back from Domino Mining which is now worth several times that figure. You, me and Ronnie will then be able to enjoy £2m each."

"We could afford a really special holiday, Raena."

"I'm one step ahead of you on that one, Chris. We'll be able to afford to stay the whole week at Bush Farm."

Ronnie White picked up the letter off the hall floor by the front door. No stamp, he thought to himself. Who's this from? Opening the envelope he took out and unfolded the page of typewritten text. Just as he was about to start reading the note he noticed in the envelope what looked like a cheque. Ronnie's first thoughts were which practical joker had made a cheque out for £2m and posted it through his letterbox? Ronnie read the note.

Hi Ron,

Hope you're keeping well. You've no doubt heard the news about those diamonds being molten pieces of glass. It's been on all the news programmes, but don't feel too bad about it. I've managed to give things the Midas touch. Enclosed my cheque for £2m. No, it's not a joke, Ron, it's your share of the reward money. You won't have to put all this money under your mattress either. It's absolutely legit, Ron, so you enjoy yourself, and thanks for the business.

Love,
Raena xx

Ronnie smiled to himself. What a girl! Ronnie looked again at Raena's cheque and said out loud, "Raena, you're definitely my kind of girl!"

At Birmingham Central, following DI Goode's transfer to Leicester, they were beginning to feel the pressure. The file on the diamond robbery whilst not closed had been shelved. Two murders in Sheldon had taken precedence over everything that week. Greg was busy interviewing three possible witnesses, and Sheila was about to go and interview a women who, according to Sergeant Ryan, claimed to know exactly what had happened. Grabbing her raincoat from the back of the chair she was about to make her way down to the car park when her internal phone rang. It was Superintendent Davies. "I know you're busy, Sheila, but you might be pleased to learn we have an extra pair of hands joining us tomorrow. Inspector Jim Houghton will be moving over from Special Branch."

Bloody hell, thought Sheila, what with him and Greg, the Jeykll and Hyde will make a fortune!

Lightning Source UK Ltd.
Milton Keynes UK
UKOW04f0052080214

226125UK00001B/30/P